He was gorgeous.

No, that didn't describe it. She needed a better word to explain how beautiful he was—but in a totally masculine way. Was it his eyes—deep brown, thickly lashed and sensual? Was it the firm set of his mouth, the perfect cheekbones, the dark hair? Was it the combination of features, the determination in his expression?

Did it matter?

He only got better as he got closer. She'd seen his pictures in magazines, but those glossy images were nothing when compared with the real thing. Billie did her best to catch her breath and act normal but her heart beat at a speed approaching Mach 3 and showed no signs of slowing.

"Congratulations," the *über*hunk said as he held out his hand. "You maneuver your jet like a pro."

"I *am* a pro." She took his hand. And nearly swooned at the sparks that arced between them....

Dear Reader,

Well, the wait is over—*New York Times* bestselling author Diana Palmer is back, and Special Edition has got her! In *Carrera's Bride*, another in Ms. Palmer's enormously popular LONG, TALL TEXANS miniseries, an innocent Jacobsville girl on a tropical getaway finds herself in need of protection—and gets it from an infamous casino owner who is not all that he appears! I think you'll find this one was well worth the wait....

We're drawing near the end of our in-series continuity THE PARKS EMPIRE. This month's entry is *The Marriage Act* by Elissa Ambrose, in which a shy secretary learns that her one night of sleeping with the enemy has led to unexpected consequences. Next up is *The Sheik & the Princess Bride* by Susan Mallery, in which a woman hired to teach a prince how to fly finds herself *his* student, as well, as he gives her lessons...in love! In *A Baby on the Ranch*, part of Stella Bagwell's popular MEN OF THE WEST miniseries, a single mother-to-be finds her long-lost family—and, just possibly, the love of her life. And a single man in the market for household help finds himself about to take on the role of husband—and father of four—in Penny Richards's *Wanted: One Father*. Oh, and speaking of single parents—a lonely widow with a troubled adolescent son finds the solution to both her problems in her late husband's law-enforcement partner, in *The Way to a Woman's Heart* by Carol Voss.

So enjoy, and come back next month for six wonderful selections from Silhouette Special Edition.

Happy Thanksgiving!

Gail Chasan
Senior Editor

Please address questions and book requests to:
Silhouette Reader Service
U.S.: 3010 Walden Ave., P.O. Box 1325, Buffalo, NY 14269
Canadian: P.O. Box 609, Fort Erie, Ont. L2A 5X3

The Sheik &
the Princess Bride

SUSAN MALLERY

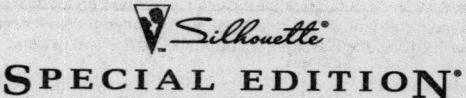

SPECIAL EDITION

Published by Silhouette Books

America's Publisher of Contemporary Romance

To Sharon. Because every woman deserves
a little fantasy in her life. This one's for you.

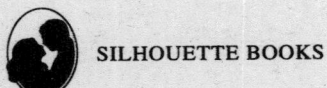 SILHOUETTE BOOKS

ISBN 0-373-24647-1

THE SHEIK & THE PRINCESS BRIDE

Copyright © 2004 by Susan Macias Redmond

This edition published by arrangement with Harlequin Books S.A.

Visit Silhouette Books at www.eHarlequin.com

Printed in U.S.A.

Books by Susan Mallery

Silhouette Special Edition

Tender Loving Care #717
More Than Friends #802
A Dad for Billie #834
Cowboy Daddy #898
*The Best Bride #933
*Marriage on Demand #939
*Father in Training #969
The Bodyguard & Ms. Jones #1008
*Part-Time Wife #1027
Full-Time Father #1042
*Holly and Mistletoe #1071
*Husband by the Hour #1099
†The Girl of His Dreams #1118
†The Secret Wife #1123
†The Mysterious Stranger #1130
The Wedding Ring Promise #1190
Prince Charming, M.D. #1209
The Millionaire Bachelor #1220
‡Dream Bride #1231
‡Dream Groom #1244
Beth and the Bachelor #1263
Surprise Delivery #1273
A Royal Baby on the Way #1281
A Montana Mavericks Christmas:
  "Married in Whitehorn" #1286
Their Little Princess #1298
**The Sheik's Kidnapped Bride #1316
**The Sheik's Arranged Marriage #1324
**The Sheik's Secret Bride #1331
‡‡The Rancher Next Door #1358
‡‡Unexpectedly Expecting! #1370
‡‡Wife in Disguise #1383
Shelter in a Soldier's Arms #1400
***The Sheik and the Runaway
  Princess* #1430
Christmas in Whitehorn #1435
**The Sheik & the Virgin Princess #1453
**The Prince & the Pregnant Princess #1473
Good Husband Material #1501
The Summer House:
  "Marrying Mandy" #1510
*Completely Smitten #1520
*One in a Million #1543
*Quinn's Woman #1557
A Little Bit Pregnant #1573
Expecting! #1585
**The Sheik & the Princess in Waiting #1606
**The Sheik & the Princess Bride #1647

Silhouette Intimate Moments

Tempting Faith #554
The Only Way Out #646
Surrender in Silk #770
Cinderella for a Night #1029

Silhouette Books

36 Hours
The Rancher and the Runaway Bride

Montana Mavericks Weddings
"Cowgirl Bride"

World's Most Eligible Bachelors
Lone Star Millionaire

Sheiks of Summer
"The Sheik's Virgin"

Harlequin Books

*Montana Mavericks:
  Big Sky Grooms*
"Spirit of the Wolf"

Harlequin Historicals

Justin's Bride #270
Wild West Wife #419
Shotgun Grooms #575
"Lucas's Convenient Bride"

**Hometown Heartbreakers
†Triple Trouble
‡Brides of Bradley House
**Desert Rogues
‡‡Lone Star Canyon

SUSAN MALLERY

is the bestselling and award-winning author of over fifty books for Harlequin and Silhouette Books. She makes her home in the Los Angeles area with her handsome prince of a husband and her two adorable-but-not-bright cats. Feel free to contact her via her Web site at www.susanmallery.com.

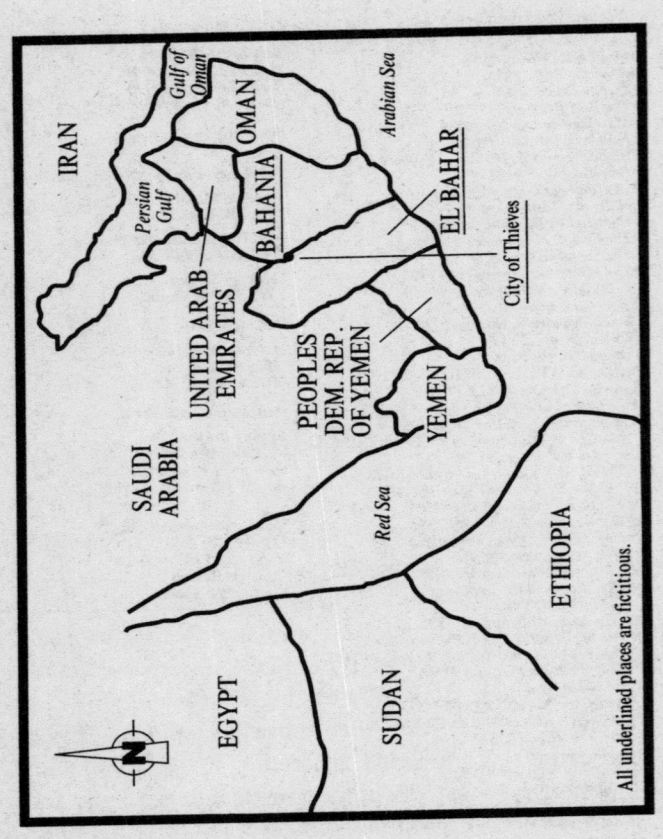

IRAN

Gulf of Oman

OMAN

Arabian Sea

Persian Gulf

BAHANIA

EL BAHAR

City of Thieves

UNITED ARAB EMIRATES

PEOPLES DEM. REP. OF YEMEN

YEMEN

SAUDI ARABIA

Red Sea

ETHIOPIA

EGYPT

SUDAN

N

All underlined places are fictitious.

Chapter One

Prince Jefri of Bahania refused to believe he could be beaten by a woman. It was simply not possible. Yet here he sat in the cockpit of his F15, going over five hundred miles an hour and staring into the sun where he'd last seen the other plane soar out of sight.

"You'd better get moving, big guy."

The amused *female* voice came through his headset and caused him to grind his teeth.

Where was she? He turned his head, searching for a glimmer of sunlight on metal. Something. Anything that would give him a clue as to her whereabouts. He saw nothing.

Jefri had been flying since he was a teenager and in all that time, he'd never once been anything but confident. For the first time in his life, he felt a cold sweat trickle down his back. Seconds later a high-pitched warning tone sounded in the cockpit. She'd locked on to him. Had this been a real combat situation, he would be dead.

"Bang, bang," the woman said and then chuckled. "You lasted all of two minutes. Not bad for a rookie. Okay. Follow me down."

Suddenly her jet swooped in from his left. The machine turned gracefully, then moved in front of his. Even at this speed, she was close enough for him to read the call sign painted on the fuselage.

Girly Girl.

Jefri groaned. This could *not* be happening. He was a prince, a sheik, heir to untold wealth and land. He was the youngest son of the king of Bahania. He did *not* get shot out of the sky by a woman!

"I know what you're thinking," she said. "You're upset and humiliated. You men always are. Console yourself with the fact that no one's beaten me in a dogfight for six or seven years. This is war, not personal. My job is to make you better. Your job is to learn. Nothing more."

"I am aware of my responsibilities," he said curtly.

"You're going to hold a grudge, aren't you? I can already tell." She sighed. "Some guys are like that. Oh, well. It's your ulcer."

With that, her jet rotated as gracefully as a ballerina, then streaked across the sky. Jefri stared at the space where it had been just a heartbeat ago. How the hell had she done that?

He shook his head and keyed in the code for the

recently installed military air traffic control tower. After giving his number and approximate position in the desert, he requested permission to return to the base. When it was granted, he turned his plane to the correct coordinates and headed south.

Twenty minutes later, he landed and taxied his jet toward the large, newly constructed hangars. When he'd stopped the plane and opened the hatch, he heard someone call his name.

"Two minutes," Doyle Van Horn yelled from the tarmac. "That's the record so far. Good for you."

Good? Jefri gritted his teeth and climbed down the ladder. "It was a disaster."

When he reached the ground, Doyle slapped him on the shoulder. "You can't take it personally. Nobody beats Billie."

"That's what she said." Jefri stared at the blond man. "How long has she been with your firm?"

Doyle grinned. "Technically, all her life. She's my sister. Dad had her driving tanks by the time she was twelve. She soloed in a jet on her sixteenth birthday. You said you wanted to be trained by the best, and that's what we provided, Your Highness."

"Call me Jefri. I've told you, no formalities. It will be easier that way."

Doyle nodded. "Just checking. I thought you might be touchy after being shot down and all. Some guys are."

Jefri didn't doubt it. He watched as a second aircraft came in for landing. The jet moved lightly, barely raising any dust when the wheels touched down.

"I wish to meet her," he said firmly.

"I figured you would. They always do."

Jefri raised his eyebrows. "Do they?"

"Yup. No one can believe it. Things only get worse when they get a look at her."

"In what way?"

Doyle laughed and held up his hands in a gesture of surrender. "You go find out for yourself. Just one warning. You might be a prince and the guy who hired us, but Billie is off-limits. To everyone. Even you."

Jefri was not used to being given orders, but he didn't argue with Doyle. He wasn't interested in Billie Van Horn as anything but a resource. If she was the best, he wanted to learn from her. Then he would take her on again, and this time he would win.

Billie climbed out of the cockpit and tugged on the zipper of her flight suit. No matter how many times she sent the manufacturer her measurements, they always got the fit wrong. Whoever designed the stupid things seemed to forget women had parts men didn't.

She jumped the last couple of feet to the ground and removed her helmet. As she did, she saw a tall man striding toward her. She recognized the determined pace, the stubborn set of the shoulders. Oh, yeah, this would be Prince Jefri. No doubt Bahanian royalty weren't used to losing. Well, he'd better *get* used to it. She didn't plan to treat him any differently than any other client, which meant he was going to keep on hearing that tone-lock for the rest of her time here.

Men always hated being beaten by her. They couldn't seem to accept that a woman could be good in a dogfight. In her experience the men she trained fell into two camps. The first got angry and aggressive, often attempting to take out their frustrations in the air by bullying and intimidating her on the ground. The second kind ignored her. Outside of the classroom or an airplane, she simply didn't exist.

A few men—a very few—saw her as an actual person and were pleasant.

But no one she'd ever trained had bothered to see her as a woman. She supposed it was asking too much to find a man who could accept that she could whip his butt in the air and still want to go dancing on Saturday night.

Prince Jefri continued to stalk closer and she wondered which camp he would fall in. Was it too much to ask that he be one of the nice guys? Did royal sheiks get trained in manners these days? Were there—

The man in question pulled off his helmet and whipped off his sunglasses as he approached. At that exact second, Billie's brain shut down.

He was gorgeous.

No, that didn't describe it. She needed a better word to explain how beautiful he was—but in a totally masculine way. Was it his eyes—deep brown, thickly lashed and sensual? Was it the firm set of his mouth, the perfect cheekbones, the dark hair? Was it the combination of features, the determination in his expression?

Did it matter?

He only got better as he got closer. She'd seen his pictures in magazines, but those glossy images were nothing when compared with the real thing. She did her best to catch her breath and act normal but her heart beat at a speed approaching Mach 3 and showed no signs of slowing.

"Congratulations," the über-hunk said as he held out his hand. "You maneuver your jet like a pro."

He sounded gracious and not the least bit put out. Was that possible?

"I *am* a pro."

She took the offered hand automatically and nearly swooned at the sparks that arced between them. She could feel them, and yet the man gently squeezing her fingers didn't seem the least bit affected. So typical, she thought with wry amusement. Something about being in the cockpit of a jet seemed to render her genderless. Ah, well. In her next life she would be a sex kitten. In this one she was destined to be permanently single.

"How did you disappear into the sun so quickly?" he asked. "I was watching. You were there and then you were gone."

"Every jet has blind spots. The trick is to know where they are and use them to your advantage."

"But I could have turned such that the blind spot moved."

She shook her head as she pulled her hand free. "You were stiff up there. I knew you'd stay on course long enough for me to get lost in the sun. Now, if you'll excuse me…"

Billie turned and headed for the temporary barracks set up at the edge of the airport. If she'd thought she would lose the man of the hour by walking quickly, she was wrong. His long stride easily kept pace with hers, and he continued to pepper her with questions. She answered his queries automatically, all the while doing her best not to notice that he fit the "tall, dark and handsome" cliché perfectly. Pretty and a prince, and about a hundred times more interested in flying than in her.

"This is my stop," she said brightly, cutting him off in mid-pound-thrust ratio question, as they reached the flap of her semipermanent home. "We'll have plenty of time to discuss all of this during the lecture time, and in simulation."

"When will I fly against you again?" he asked.

She tugged the zipper of her flight suit down to her hips and pulled her arms free of the heavy fabric. It might be October in the desert, but it was still warm. She plucked at the T-shirt she wore underneath.

"We'll have plenty of air time," she told him. "Don't worry, I'll be killing you over and over again."

"I think not. About that last maneuver…"

The man didn't even notice she had breasts, Billie thought with a combination of humor and regret. She'd often thought she could step out of her flight suit and walk around stark naked and not one of the pilots would notice. Of course her brothers would see and probably kill her.

"I'm off duty until the morning," she said politely, wishing she could give him a gentle push back to his palace or wherever it was he lived. "I know you're anxious, what with getting your new air force up and running, but I don't work 24/7. Call me crazy."

With that she disappeared into the tent.

Jefri frowned. Had the female instructor turned her back on him and walked away? He followed her inside. "You don't understand. I need this information," he said, barely noticing the Spartan setting.

Billie glanced at him, then smiled. "You don't give up, do you?"

"No."

She opened the drawer of a dresser and pulled out several garments, then disappeared behind a screen.

"Okay, fly boy. I'll give you fifteen minutes, but then you have to let me get some rest. I flew all night to get here and my regular tent isn't set up yet. I'm stuck in regulation housing until then. No offense, but it's hot here and I want my air-conditioning. Oh, have a seat."

He glanced around for a chair and saw one in the corner. There was a small ball in the seat. As he reached for it, the ball moved, uncoiled, growled and snapped at him.

From behind the screen, he heard laughter.

"I see you found Muffin."

He eyed the ball of fur with distaste. "Muffin?"

''My baby. Be nice to the tall man, sweetie,'' Billie said. ''He's paying the bills. Just go ahead and scratch under her chin. Oh, and tell her she's pretty. Muffin likes that.''

Jefri eyed the tiny dog. All he saw was multicolored strands of hair and two mistrustful eyes. Hardly anything attractive.

''Get down,'' he said and pointed to the floor of the tent.

Muffin made a sound very much like a huff, turned her back on him and curled up in a ball. On the chair. He reached for her, but before he could pick her up, she growled.

''I would kill for a bath,'' Billie said with a sigh, and Jefri allowed himself to be distracted. ''But we don't actually travel with a tub. Doyle says it's too inconvenient. Oh, sure, we can move millions of pounds of jets and computer equipment with no problem, but one lousy tub is difficult. What is it with guys? Why don't you get the whole point of a nice long soak?''

As she spoke she stepped out from behind the screen. Jefri began to answer, when his senses went on alert. For the first time since she'd climbed down from the jet he actually *looked* at her.

Girly girl didn't begin to describe things.

She was a centerfold fantasy come to life—big blond hair, big blue eyes and bigger breasts. Her sundress hugged her impressive curves before falling to midthigh. High-heeled sandals gave her a little height, but she still barely cleared his shoulder.

After giving him a smile bright enough to be listed as an energy source, she crossed to the fur ball and gathered it in her arms.

"How's my pretty girl?" she asked in a baby voice. "Did you say hello to the nice prince?"

Billie held the dog's paw in her hand and gave it a little wave. "Muffin says hi."

Prince Jefri of Bahania had never had anyone pretend to speak for an animal before. He glanced from the woman to the dog and back.

Billie grinned. "Okay, so you're not a 'talk to the animals' kind of guy. I can accept that. Doyle swears he hates her but I see him sneaking her treats every now and then."

She walked toward the tent flap and pushed it open. "I thought it would be cooler here, given the time of year. I guess not, though. It's the desert and all." Still cuddling the dog, she walked out into the sunlight. "Not to be too pushy, but your time is ticking away. Didn't you have more questions to ask me?"

Questions? Jefri followed her out, then saw the rows of fighter jets. Yes, of course. He'd had dozens of things he wanted to know, but he couldn't think of any of them. Not when the hem of her form-fitting dress drew his gaze to her perfect thighs, and the sway of her hips made his blood boil.

He was unused to such strong physical reactions. Women had always been easy for him. He saw, he wanted, he was offered. But Billie seemed oblivious to her appeal, nor did she see him as more than an eager student.

She spun around and faced him. "What?" she asked, her blue eyes wide with amusement. "I know I haven't intimidated you, so out with it. What do you want to know?"

He had a thousand requests for information. How soft would her skin feel under his fingers? How would she taste when he kissed her? How low would she moan as he pleasured her over and over, because his fantasies about Billie were about making her surrender with desire?

"Why do you do this?" he asked. "Why do you fly?"

"Because I love it. I've always loved it." She grinned. "And I'm damned good at it."

"Yes, you are."

Two airplane mechanics walked by. Both of them eyed Billie. They bent their heads together and exchanged words he couldn't hear. But he could imagine.

Jefri looked at the large tents, the open camp and then back at Billie. This would not do.

"You cannot stay here," he told her.

Her smile faded. "Excuse me? You're throwing me out of your country?"

"No. Of course not. I'm saying you can't stay in this camp. It's not safe."

Her good humor returned. "I appreciate the concern, but I've been living in camps just like this since I was eleven. They're a little rough on the outside, but still plenty fun. It's sweet of you to worry, but you don't have to. I usually have three brothers and a father hanging around. This time there's only Doyle, but he's plenty burly and he'll make sure I'm well protected.'' She rubbed her cheek against the dog's shoulder. ''Too protected. Isn't that right, little Muffin girl?''

He ignored her conversation with the dog. ''You and your brother will be my guests in the palace.''

She blinked at him. ''Did you say palace?''

''Yes. There are several dozen guest rooms. You would be very comfortable there.''

''Do these rooms have bathtubs?'' Temptation thickened her voice.

''Large enough to swim in.''

She made a low noise in her throat. The sound made his blood surge.

''Gee, a real bed, walls, a roof and a sand-free life,'' she said. ''Color me there. Doyle objects, I'll have to deck him.''

''This is a complete waste of time if you ask me,'' Doyle muttered as the long, black limo drove between large wrought-iron gates. ''We've never stayed with a client before.''

Billie gazed out at the extensive and well-manicured lawns. ''We've never had a royal client before. It's a palace, okay? This is a once-in-a-lifetime opportunity. No one's forcing you to suffer through the indignities of pure luxury. Go back to our tent city by the airport if it makes you happy.''

Her brother glared at her. ''You know Dad would kill me if I wasn't around to keep an eye on you.''

"I'm twenty-seven, Doyle," she said. "At some point you're going to have to acknowledge that I'm all grown-up."

"Ain't gonna happen."

She shook her head at the familiar sentiment. It was hard enough being the baby of the family, but being the only girl made things worse.

Still, she'd gotten used to their high-handed treatment years ago and for the most part was able to ignore it. When she didn't care one way or another, she usually gave in. But not this time. Not when there was a bathtub on the line.

The car rounded a corner and Billie felt her eyes widen. "I can't believe it," she breathed as she took in the multistory pink palace sprawling in front of her.

The main building was huge—the size of a museum or a parliament building. Balconies circled every floor. There were turrets and arched windows and guards on the ground and lush gardens for as far as the eye could see.

"Not bad," Doyle said.

Billie cuffed him. "You're impressed. It's amazing. Too bad Dad and the guys can't be here to see it."

Her father was in South America attending a multinational conference and her two oldest brothers had special assignments in Iraq. Which left Doyle and her in charge of the Bahanian job. Easy work, Billie thought. She could train an air force pilot in her sleep. Flying was something she loved and one of the few things she did well.

The limo pulled to a stop and a uniformed guard

stepped forward to open the rear door. Doyle stepped out first. Billie grabbed Muffin and slid across the slick, leather seat. As she stepped out into the sunlight, her eyes took a second to adjust. During that second or two, her gaze landed on Prince Jefri and she would have sworn she saw him bathed in shimmering gold.

Neat trick, she thought as her mind whirled from the beauty of the palace and her body swooned from the beauty of the man.

"Ms. Van Horn." The prince nodded.

"Billie," she said with a smile. "As I'm going to be shooting you out of the sky on a regular basis, there's no point in being formal."

She thought the prince might have winced at her words. No doubt he thought he would get good enough to win against her. They all thought that, and they were all wrong. Which meant he would get more and more crabby as the training went along. Oh, well. It had happened before and she had survived.

The prince spoke to a uniformed young woman who nodded, then gestured toward Doyle. Her brother gave Billie a quick wink as he followed the maid into the castle. Billie stepped up for her escort and tried not to drool at the thought of the riches within.

"This way," Prince Jefri said.

She blinked at him. "Excuse me?"

"I will show you to your room."

Did royalty do that? She figured about the only thing a prince did for himself was breathe. Hadn't she read somewhere that some royals even had a special servant to put toothpaste on the toothbrush?

"You don't have to do that yourself," she said, thinking of her bath and how long she was going to soak. At least an hour. She had a good book she wanted to finish and a...

"Is this your first visit to my country?" he asked.

"Um, yes." She shifted Muffin to her other arm and trailed along beside the prince. "I wasn't part of the sales presentation when our firm bid for the training job."

They entered into a foyer the size of a small arena. The gold inlaid ceilings soared a good fifty feet above them. Mosaics of ancient battles lined the curved walls. Not exactly like the flocked wallpaper in that hotel in Bosnia.

He noticed her interest and paused in front of a mural of several fierce men on horses. "My people have always been fighters. A thousand years ago, we defended our land against the infidels."

She looked at him out of the corner of her eye. "That would be us, right?"

"Only if you are European."

"I'm a bit of everything." She looked at the elaborate chandelier and the stained glass windows. "Beautiful place."

"Thank you. The Pink Palace is a treasure for the people of Bahania."

"How many of them get to stay here on a regular basis?"

The prince surprised her by smiling. "We hold it in trust."

"I'm sure they're grateful."

He started down the main hallway. Billie followed, noting they could have easily driven a tank and not come close to bumping into any walls.

"I did some research before I got here," she said, her high-heeled sandals clicking loudly on the tiled floor. "Your country is not strictly Muslim."

"No. Our people celebrate many faiths, and respect all."

That's what all her reading had told her. While the rest of the Middle East couldn't seem to get it together, Bahania, and their neighbor El Bahar, offered religious freedom to all. The monarchies had ruled for over a thousand years with no hint of uprising. Ultimate power that didn't corrupt? Was it possible?

"So why the air force?" she asked.

"To protect our oil fields. With so much unrest around us, we need to be able to secure our resources."

"The oil won't last forever."

"True, which is why even now we are diversifying our exports. Bahania will not be left behind in the world market."

Pretty *and* smart, she thought with a little smile. Now if only he could see her as a desirable woman, her life would be complete. Her research had informed her that Prince Jefri was single, but she'd seen pictures of the women in his life. There wasn't a fighter pilot in the bunch.

They passed room after room. Some were decorated with elegant Western-style furniture while others had low sofas and cushions, more suited to a nomadic tent. There were paintings and frescos and statues and...

Muffin squirmed in her arms.

"What is it sweetie?" she asked.

The dog yipped and squirmed some more. Seconds later a large white cat strolled out of a meeting room large enough to hold the entire Congress.

Billie yelped and clutched her dog more tightly to her chest. "What is that?" she asked as she took a step back.

The prince stared at her. "A cat," he said with the obvious patience of one speaking to a mentally challenged person.

Annoyance overcame hormones and she glared at him. "I *know* it's a cat. What's it doing here?"

"My father has an affection for cats."

She eyed the fluffy white demon. "I read that but I thought more in the lines of a painting on velvet or some carvings. Are you telling me there are actual cats in the palace?"

"Dozens. Is that a problem?"

She saw the corner of the prince's mouth twitch, as if he was amused by her reaction.

"I'm not a cat person."

"They will not hurt you."

She wasn't all that sure. If there were dozens, they could gang up on her and take her down. "What about Muffin?"

"I'm sure your...dog will be safe."

She didn't like how he said ''dog'' and she didn't like the cats.

''Do you have an allergy?'' he asked.

''Not exactly.''

''Then what, exactly?''

''I had a bad experience when I was young.''

''With a small lion?''

She narrowed her gaze. Suddenly he wasn't nearly as handsome and not the least bit intelligent. ''Would you like to show me to my room?''

''More than life itself.''

Chapter Two

Jefri could tell his guest was annoyed and unhappy about the cats. While he didn't appreciate them as his father did, especially when they shed on all the furniture and covered his clothes in cat hair, they were little more than a mild inconvenience. But watching Billie Van Horn skitter around them, jump away and generally act as if she was in mortal danger every time one of them crossed her path, he wondered what possible trauma in her past could have caused such an overreaction.

At least wondering about her cat phobia gave him something to think about other than the perfection of her body. She was all lush curves and earthy appeal. Her scent—soap, something floral and a hint of the woman herself—made his blood heat. He wouldn't have minded his reaction if she'd been trying to get his attention, but she seemed to be far more concerned about protecting herself from marauding felines.

He led the way to an elevator that took them to the third floor. When the doors opened, a tabby sat in the middle of the hallway. Billie jumped which, considering her high-heeled sandals, made him worry for the state of her slender ankles.

"Were you attacked?" he asked as she sidled around the twelve-pound feline.

"What?" She glanced at him, her blue eyes wide with worry. "Not me, but a close friend." She pressed her lips together. "Muffin is only seven pounds. They could slice her to ribbons and serve her for breakfast."

Jefri thought of how much time his father's cats spent sleeping. "I doubt they are that ambitious."

Billie's sniff told him she wasn't impressed by his logic.

As much as he wanted her in the palace, he hadn't intended his invitation to distress her.

"Would you prefer to stay at the barracks?"

She shook her head. "We'll manage."

"The room is just up there."

He motioned to a door, then stepped ahead of her to open it. Billie stepped inside and her breath caught in an audible gasp. Jefri followed her gaze, taking in the large living area, the floor-to-ceiling windows offering a view of the Arabian Sea and the wide double doors that led to the sleeping quarters.

"Will you be comfortable here?" he asked politely.

"Yes. And should I feel the need to take in boarders to supplement my income, there will be plenty of room." She grinned. "This I could get used to."

"You may consider the palace your home while you're in Bahania."

"You might want to be careful with an invitation like that. What if I never want to leave?"

Then she would be available to him whenever he wanted. Jefri turned the thought over in his mind and found it gave him pleasure. Too bad his father had done away with the harem. She would have been a wonderful addition.

"Please let any of the staff know if you have any needs," he said instead of telling her what he was really thinking.

"Sure thing. I can't imagine needing anything else, though. This room is amazing."

She bent over and set her dog on the floor. The fur ball trotted to the sofa and began sniffing at the furniture.

"Do you always travel with your pet?" Jefri asked.

"Yup. Muffin and I are a package deal. I've even taken her up flying with me."

He couldn't imagine why. "Does she enjoy it?"

"Hard to tell," Billie admitted. "She doesn't throw up, so that's something."

Wanting to talk about something other than the creature touring the room, he crossed to the French doors and pointed toward the sea.

"The balcony circles the entire palace. From the south end you can look toward Lucia-Serrat."

"I've heard of the island. It's supposed to be very beautiful."

"Much of this area is."

She shook her head. "I had a mental picture of sand as far as the eye could see. But the city sprawls over a much bigger area than I would have thought. Of course when it ends, there *are* miles of sand."

"You noticed that while you were flying today?"

She nodded. "Not much else to do up there. The first few days of dogfighting are pretty boring what with…"

Her voice trailed off. He saw her swallow, then she glanced at him from under long lashes.

"So that was bad, right?" she asked, sounding more resigned than contrite. "I've just insulted a prince. Is there a punishment? Do I get sent to the dungeon?"

"Why the sudden concern?" he asked. "Back at the airport you told me I would never beat you."

"Oh, you won't," she told him. "But I should probably be more subtle about it all."

"Because of the palace?"

"It does sort of put our lives in perspective. I'm a small-town girl and you're…not."

"Indeed. I would not even qualify as a big-city girl."

Her beautiful mouth twisted. "You know what I mean. Maybe you could get me a brochure or some notes. Something along the lines of twenty ways not to insult royalty."

"There is a person in charge of etiquette. Perhaps I should have him drop by."

Billie wrinkled her nose. "You're making fun of me."

"Only a little."

"Wow. You have a sense of humor. What's next on the surprise parade? Do you do your own laundry?"

"Never."

"A guy thing. My brothers don't do theirs either. But then that's fairly typical of—"

A sharp yowl cut through the conversation. He turned toward the sound but Billie was already moving across the marble flooring. Several sharp barks were followed by a yip.

"Muffin!" she cried as she plunged into a fray of fur, paws, teeth and tails.

While Jefri had no desire to rescue her pet, he felt obligated to offer assistance. He eyed Billie's bare legs and hands, then moved behind her, wrapped an arm around her waist and lifted her out of the way.

She squealed, adding to the din. He had a brief impression of curves, heat and potential before he set her down behind him.

"I'll take care of this," he said as he reached into the swirl of cats and plucked out a small growling, yelping ball of fur.

For his trouble he received several scratches, a bite from the dog and enough hair on his suit to change the color from black to gray.

"I believe this is yours." He handed the small, shaking dog to her.

She pulled the creature close and brushed her hands over its body. "Muffin! Are you hurt? Did those horrible, mean killers hurt you?"

After reassuring herself that Muffin had indeed survived, she turned her attention to him.

"I don't know what to say," she breathed, her blue eyes wide and anguished. "They could have killed her."

He examined his hand. Muffin's bite hadn't broken the skin, but several of the cats had left their mark.

"I think she would have survived the encounter."

He crossed to the main door and opened it, then shooed the cats out of the suite.

"There may still be one or two left in here," he said. "Just give them a push out the door."

She glanced around uneasily, then moved close. "How can I thank you?"

Her voice was low and intense. Had she been someone of his usual social circle, he would have assumed she was offering more than a polite acknowledgment of what he'd done. But with Billie, he wasn't so sure. Besides, as much as he wanted her in his bed, he intended to seduce her every step of the way. He had a feeling that with her, anticipation would only make the experience sweeter.

"It was no matter."

She shook her head and set Muffin on the sofa. "It was a huge deal. Those cats were so horrible." She reached for his hand and took it in hers. "You're bleeding!"

A few of the scratches seeped blood. Jefri wasn't the least bit concerned, but he didn't object when Billie dragged him into the large bathroom and ran water over his hand.

Her skin was smooth and warm against his own. She stood close enough for him to feel the heat of her body and the light brush of her breasts against his arm.

"You were very brave," she said.

"They were only cats."

"Killers by nature," she murmured as she reached for a towel.

He wiped his hands then touched his finger to her chin. "What happened that made you so afraid of cats? While I'll agree they are hunters, they are small enough that you would never be in danger of them."

She shrugged. "I don't like them."

"I gathered that. The question is why?"

Billie sighed. Her breath teased his skin and he dropped his hand to his side.

"When I was young, I desperately wanted a pet," she said. "Something of my own. But my mother was concerned about getting me one because my brothers were so wild. She doubted any pet big enough to hold its own with them would be a good animal for me. But on my seventh birthday, my brothers pitched in and got me a white mouse."

She smiled. "I know they did it because they

thought the mouse would scare me, but I wasn't frightened at all.''

"You have three older brothers?" he asked.

She nodded.

He thought of the size and strength of Doyle Van Horn and knew that Billie would have to have been tough to survive in that household.

"I loved Missy," Billie said.

He raised his eyebrows. "Missy the Mouse?"

"Uh-huh. She was very sweet and tame. I taught her tricks."

"Such as?"

"She knew her name and she would stand on her back legs when I offered her food."

"That's not a trick. She was simply attempting to reach the food."

Billie's eyes narrowed. "She was *my* mouse. I get to say if it was a trick or not."

"Fair enough. So you had this mouse. I suspect there was a cat involved."

Billie nodded. She leaned against the bathroom counter. "We had this playroom. There was a latch up higher than I could reach and sometimes, if I slammed the door, it locked into place. One day Missy got out. I couldn't find her anywhere. I wanted my brothers to help me find her, but they wouldn't. I was mad, so I stomped into the playroom and slammed the door. It locked behind me."

Her voice remained firm, but he heard the edge of emotion. Why? Over the death of a mouse twenty years ago? What possible reason could she have for caring?

Billie folded her arms over her chest. "I walked to the window and looked out and that's when I saw Missy. Two of the neighbor's cats had her cornered. They were playing with her. Torturing her. I screamed for my brothers to let me out but they were in the front yard and couldn't hear me. My mom was at the grocery store. I was trapped for nearly two hours. That's about how long it took them to kill and eat her."

Jefri winced. "You didn't turn away?"

"How could I? She was my mouse." She sighed. "I remember sobbing and my mom finding me. She tried to convince me it hadn't been Missy, but how many white mice live in the wild?"

"So that is why you dislike cats?"

"Wouldn't you?"

He couldn't imagine having a mouse as a pet in the first place. "They were acting on instinct, not out of malice."

"Oh, and that makes Missy's death acceptable?"

"Of course not." Were they really talking about a mouse?

"It's hard having pets," she said as she straightened her arms and pushed off the counter. "But worth it. Now I have Muffin and I'm going to make sure nothing bad ever happens to her. No palace cat is going to be allowed to have her for dinner."

"The cats here are well fed."

"They'd better be."

Temper flashed in her eyes. Jefri wondered how they'd shifted topics so completely. Given his choice they would be talking about flying or how attractive she found him. So far they had done neither.

"I will tell the staff to keep the cats out of your rooms as much as possible," he said.

"Really? That would be great." She glanced at the tub. "If you hadn't tempted me with such a great bathroom, I probably would have returned to the barracks. But this is pretty irresistible."

Ah, so she could resist him, but not a bathtub. That put things in perspective.

"About your stay here," he said, deciding flying was the safest topic. "You will have to be at the airport each day?"

"Yup. There's plenty of butt for me to kick in your nice blue skies."

"I'm sure my men will enjoy learning from you," he told her, ignoring the assumption that she would continue to best him. He was going to make sure that didn't happen.

"Oh, they're going to learn, whether they enjoy the process or not."

"I will put a car and driver at your disposal. Simply tell the driver where you wish to go and he will take you there."

Her mouth parted. "You're kidding? My own driver?"

"You may share him if you would like."

She laughed. "No, that's okay. As I said before, I could really get used to this."

"I hope you'll enjoy your stay in my country."

He nodded at her and left. While there was much more to be said, this wasn't the time. Later, when he'd decided on his strategy he would talk to her about more than her work. He would discover the secrets of the beautiful woman who flew like a falcon and moved with the grace of the cats she found so distasteful. He would learn her strengths, her weaknesses and he would have her in his bed. He would also best her in the air. To be honest, he wasn't sure which he would enjoy more.

Billie finished drying her hair and stepped back to admire the effect. "Not bad," she murmured to her reflection, as she fluffed up a curl. She'd always been a big-hair kind of gal and the complete lack of humidity in Bahania meant no risk of her carefully poofed style going flat.

Nearly an hour in a massive tub had relaxed her. Now rested, redressed in a sundress and still jet-lagged from her trip the previous day she felt both tired and antsy.

"We should take a walk," she told Muffin as she moved back into the living room of the suite. "A couple of laps in this room would almost do it, huh?"

She grinned as she spoke, then turned in a circle as she admired the elegant Western-style furnishings and beautiful paintings. There was a thick oriental rug by the sofa and a dining area to the left. The view was as spectacular as any she'd ever seen from the ground.

Silent air-conditioning kept the room a comfortable seventy-six degrees.

"The good life," she said as she gathered Muffin in her arms. "Okay, what if we take a quick walk outside, then figure out what we're doing about dinner? I mean does the palace have room service? I should have asked the prince about it."

She would have, too, if he hadn't been so tall and princely while he'd showed her around the suite.

"The man is a hunk," she told her little dog as she carried her out into the corridor. "Wish he were my type."

Not that Billie had an actual type. That would require a level of involvement she'd never had.

"In my next life I'll be a guy magnet," she told herself. "They'll be tripping over each other to get to me."

But until then, it was just her and her dog.

Billie walked to the end of the corridor and took the stairs down. She had a good sense of direction and was able to find her way to the garden in under five minutes.

The lush cultivated space seemed larger at ground level. The various gardens spilled into each other, more formal English garden hedges giving way to serene pools surrounded by tropical disarray. She set Muffin down, careful to keep an eye on her so she wasn't cornered and attacked by marauding cats.

"Not bad," Billie murmured as Muffin began to sniff. "Easy to understand why it's good to be the prince."

Her sandals clicked loudly on the stone path. She wove her way between plants and bushes and trees, stopping to smell a flower or finger a leaf. She didn't know all that much about growing things. Her expertise required an engine and enough thrust and speed to break the sound barrier. Still, if one had to stay earthbound, this was the place.

She rounded a corner and saw a man sitting on a bench. He looked up as she approached, then stood.

"Good afternoon," he said with a smile. "Who might you be?"

The man was tall and handsome, albeit older. Gray spread from his temples and there were lines by his dark, deep-set eyes. His well-tailored suit reminded her of a bank president or senator, not that she'd ever met either.

"Billie Van Horn," she said, holding out her hand.

"Ah, the military expert. I recognize the name." He shook hands with her, then motioned to the bench. "You are a member of the family?"

"The only girl. A giant pain, let me tell you." She settled on one end of the stone bench while he took the other. "The good news is I'm a great pilot and if my brothers ever make me too crazy I challenge them to a dogfight." She grinned. "A fighter jet is a great equalizer."

"I can imagine."

Muffin trotted up and sniffed at the nice man's shoes.

"My dog," Billie said. "Muffin. I'd heard there

were cats, but I didn't expect so many. I'm trying to keep Muffin from being the chef's special.''

''I doubt you have to worry. She looks capable of taking care of herself.''

''Not when she's outnumbered. There was already a fight in my room.''

The older man raised his eyebrows. ''You are staying at the palace?''

''Yes. Prince Jefri invited me and my brother Doyle.'' She leaned close. ''I confess I was seduced by the thought of a bathtub. Roughing it comes with the job, so how could I resist a few weeks in a palace? The place is amazing.''

''I'm glad you think so.''

A cat strolled up. Billie eyed it with distaste but her companion simply stroked its back.

''You fly jets?'' he asked. ''That is your job?''

''I do most of the in-air training. I also work with the pilots on the simulators. It's fun.''

''You are good at this?''

She grinned. ''The best. This morning I blew Prince Jefri out of the sky in less than two minutes. Not literally, of course.''

''How comforting. I am not yet ready to lose my youngest son.''

As the words sank in, Billie opened her mouth, then closed it. ''S-son?'' she repeated, hoping she'd misunderstood. ''You're his father?''

''Yes.''

She looked into the dark eyes and realized the resemblance had been staring her in the face.

''But that would make you…''

''The king.''

''Oh, God.''

She half rose, thought about *The King and I* and wondered if she was allowed to hold her head higher than his. Was that a real law or just humor for a musical?

''I can't…'' She swallowed. ''I didn't…'' Giving in to the need to curl up and die, she covered her face with her hands and moaned. ''How many laws have I broken?''

''No more than three or four.''

She spread her fingers and peeked at the king. He didn't look angry. If the smile was anything to go by, he was amused.

She dropped her hands to her lap and straightened. ''You could have told me.''

''I did.''

''I mean before. When I said, 'Hi, I'm Billie.' You could have said, 'Hey, I'm the king.' ''

''This was more interesting. You would not have spoken so freely with me if you had known who I am.''

''No kidding. So do I bow or something?''

''You do neither. I am King Hassan of Bahania.'' He nodded regally. ''Welcome to my country.''

''Thank you. It's great.'' She sighed. ''I guess I'd better apologize for not liking cats.''

''Caring for them is not required, although you aren't allowed to injure any.''

''I'm okay with that, but Muffin may be another

matter.'' She glanced down at her dog and wrinkled her nose. ''She's only seven pounds, so I don't think she could do much more than cause a lot of noise.''

The king followed her gaze, then smiled. ''That is true. I will have to hope my cats are up to the challenge. If there—''

A loud howl interrupted his sentence. Billie sprang to her feet and headed toward the noise just as a black-and-white cat flew in front of her. She sidestepped to avoid stepping on the horrible creature and slid off the stone path. Her momentum didn't help her regain her balance and she felt herself falling.

Suddenly strong arms grabbed her from behind. Someone hauled her up, rescuing her from what could have been some serious pain. Billie caught her breath as she felt rock-hard muscles, incredible body heat and the thundering beat of her own heart.

Please God let her not have been rescued by the king. He was handsome and all that, but old enough that having a visceral reaction to him bordered on icky.

She turned her head and breathed a sigh of relief when she saw Jefri gazing at her from only a few inches away.

''Your dog seems to be in trouble again,'' he said as he righted her. ''She has a knack for finding it.''

Billie straightened and brushed off her dress. ''I would say with all these cats stalking her, she has little choice except to protect herself.''

Remembering the presence of the king a half sentence too late, she swallowed. "Not that the cats aren't lovely," she added in a small voice.

Jefri raised his eyebrows, but didn't speak. The king looked amused. He bent over and scooped up a now calm and silent Muffin.

"So you *are* a troublemaker," he said, staring into her dog's little face. "Perhaps you need to learn your place in the world."

Billie hoped that place didn't involve a cage. "She travels with me everywhere. She's sort of spoiled."

"So I see." He set the dog down on the ground and patted her head. "I would like you and your brother to join me for dinner tonight." He straightened. "If you can bear to leave the little one in your room."

Dinner with the king? How many times did that happen to a girl like her?

"Absolutely." She mentally flashed on her wardrobe. "Formal? Informal?"

"It will just be family," he said.

Which didn't answer her question but made her wonder if the ever-hunky Prince Jefri would be there.

"Good. Would you like to inform your brother?"

Billie thought of Doyle's reaction to dinner with royalty. He wouldn't be amused.

"I'll let you tell him," she said, knowing even *her* brother wouldn't dare lose his temper with a king. "He'll be thrilled."

Jefri's mouth twitched, which made her wonder if he knew what she was thinking.

Not possible, she told herself. Men like him didn't

care about brains or thoughts. They wanted… She paused as she realized she didn't know what men like him wanted from women. But as she was neither a supermodel nor the heir to a champagne fortune, she was unlikely to find out anytime soon.

"Seven-thirty then," the king said.

"I'll be there." She bent over and scooped up Muffin, then headed back to her room. If she was going to dine with royalty she needed much bigger hair.

Jefri finished knotting his tie and turned to reach for his jacket. As he picked it up, he checked the fabric for cat hairs.

"Try this," his brother, Murat, said and tossed him a delinting roll.

"Thanks."

Jefri went to work on his jacket while Murat lounged on the recently dehaired sofa.

"She really has a dog?" his brother asked.

"It is more of a rat with fur." Of course Billie seemed to have an affinity for rodents, he thought remembering the tragedy of her mouse.

"And she shot you out of the sky?"

Jefri shrugged into the jacket and turned his attention on his brother. "Not literally."

"I can see that." Murat grinned. "I cannot wait to meet her."

"She is…unexpected."

"Sounds interesting."

Jefri said nothing as he stared at Murat. His brother rose, stretched, then chuckled.

"I *am* the crown prince," Murat said, as if Jefri needed reminding. "I may claim who I choose."

"You may not claim this one."

One dark eyebrow rose. "Why not?"

Jefri allowed himself a small smile. "She is mine."

"Ah. Does she know?"

"Not yet, but she will. Soon."

"Then I wish you luck, my brother."

"I will not need it."

Jefri was determined. Nothing would stand in the way of his learning all of Billie's secrets, then having her in his bed.

Chapter Three

Like most women, Billie had loved to play dress-up when she'd been younger, so the chance to actually put on finery for real was too good to pass up. Plus one of her job perks was attending the Paris Air Show every other year. Which meant after she and her brothers oohed and ahhed over the latest in aviation technology, she went shopping.

She stood now in one of her impulse purchases—a shimmering floor-length dark purple gown. The halter-style permitted her to show off curves and still wear a bra—always exciting. Combs held her hair off her face and allowed her to tease the curls up about another inch, while long tendrils cascaded down her back. Strappy silver sandals with four-inch heels made her feel like an Amazon goddess…well, a short one anyway.

"What do you think?" she asked, holding out two different earrings for Muffin to inspect. Her dog lay on the high four-poster bed. "These are more dangling, but these have more flash."

Muffin barked.

"I agree. Flash over dangle," Billie said and put on the smaller cubic zirconia earrings.

After a light spritzing of perfume, she pronounced herself as ready as she was going to be.

"I promise to bring you back something," she said. "I'm sure we'll have some kind of meat dish. I tucked a Baggie in my purse." She waved her tiny evening bag at Muffin.

The trick would be getting the bit of entrée from her plate to her handbag, but she'd done it countless times before and had almost never been caught.

"Okay. You be good. I'll see you soon."

Billie pushed the play button on the DVD player in the bedroom armoire, then headed for the door. As she stepped into the hallway of the amazing pink palace, she had the feeling that for the first time in her life, she was almost a princess.

"Way better than Halloween dress-up," she murmured as she started down a corridor.

As she paused by the elevator, waiting for it to take her to the second floor because there was no way she could do stairs in these shoes or the long dress, she heard a door close and the sound of footsteps. Seconds later Jefri walked toward her.

"Good evening," he said, looking more than a little spiffy in a black tux. So she'd guessed right then, "a family dinner'' in royal circles meant way dressier than jeans.

The soft wool fabric of Jefri's tux had the faintest shimmer to it, and Billie had an instant urge to touch. That would be bad, she told herself, trying not to swoon as she took in the rest of the package.

Most men cleaned up pretty well and looked good in a tuxedo, but those who had a head start in the looks department came out looking even better. Jefri was no exception. He'd brushed his dark hair away from his face, which emphasized his stern yet handsome features. The white shirt collar and cuffs made his skin seem darker. Billie avoided the sun whenever possible. She burned more than tanned and didn't want to be fighting the leather look when she was fifty.

Knowing how pale she was and how dark he was gave her a little shiver. She had a visual of them entwined in bed, looking like actors for an erotic movie.

''Hi,'' she said and waggled her fingers. ''You look nice.''

He reached for her free hand and raised it slightly, then kissed her knuckles. ''You are enchanting. The glories of my country pale when compared to your beauty.''

Okay, sure. It was a line and little old-fashioned, but it worked. Billie felt her knees get a little wobbly and her heart start to pound.

The elevator doors opened. Jefri put his hand on her back to urge her to enter first. His thumb and forefinger landed on bare skin. Goose bumps erupted, even as warmth poured through her.

"I see you left Muffin in your room," he said.

"I thought it was best. I always feel badly when I'm going to have fun without her, but she's watching a movie."

He pushed the button for the second floor. "Excuse me? Your dog is watching a movie?"

"Uh-huh. And I have to say that DVD collection in the armoire was fabulous. I had a hard time deciding, but in the end I put on *Legally Blonde II* because she has a real thing for Bruiser. That's the dog in the movie."

Jefri's gaze never left her face, yet she felt him mentally drifting. He blinked.

"I do not understand," he told her. "You are the same woman who can fly a fighter jet better than anyone I know."

The doors opened and they stepped out.

"Yup. That's me."

"Yet you put on a movie for your *dog?*"

"I don't really see how the two concepts relate."

"Nor do I. This way."

He escorted her down a long corridor. Soft lighting spilled from the dozens of rooms they passed. Talk about a lot of space. Taking a lap around each floor would pretty much take care of anyone's aerobic needs for the day.

"I heard your brother could not join us tonight," Jefri said.

"The rest of the equipment arrived and he wanted

to oversee that. If you ask me, he was in a snit about having to get dressed up for dinner. His loss. I'm sure the food will be amazing.''

"I hope you find that everything pleases you.''

His low voice scraped along her bare skin like a length of nubby fabric. Billie felt strange, sort of trembling and overheated and spacey. She had to get a grip. In the heels she wore, one wrong step could be fatal.

They turned left at a large pillar and entered what she supposed for them was a small, casual dining room. For her it was like being asked to eat in the roped-off parts of the British Museum.

A long table stood in the center of the room. From the number of chairs pushed up against the walls, she supposed it could be expanded to seat at least thirty, maybe more. Two antique hutches stood flanking a large tapestry depicting a young woman in an open kind of boat. Based on her dress, Billie would guess the scene was from the mid-sixteen hundreds.

Three chandeliers provided light over the table, but instead of using bulbs they twinkled with candlelight. Several sconces lined the walls, also providing illumination. A long buffet held a bucket of champagne on ice and unopened bottles of red and white wine, along with an assortment of liquors. Two men with trays of canapés hovered by the doorway, and there wasn't a cat in sight.

"This works,'' Billie said as she and Jefri strolled the length of the room.

"I'm glad you like it. Champagne?''

"Sure. I'm not flying until late tomorrow morning."

Jefri popped the bottle with an ease that made her feel like an extra in an old Audrey Hepburn movie, then accepted the delicate crystal glass.

"To new adventures," he said, touching his glass to hers. "And those we share them with."

She figured this wasn't the time for her usual "Bottoms up" so she smiled before taking a sip. The liquid bubbles tickled the whole way down her throat. Oh, yeah. This was the good life for sure.

A tall man Billie hadn't met entered the dining room. Based on his good looks and regal bearing she was going to take a wild guess and say he was another royal prince.

Bingo, she thought, when Jefri introduced him as "My oldest brother, Crown Prince Murat."

She had her purse in one hand and her champagne in the other. For one horrible second, Billie thought maybe she was expected to curtsey. Why hadn't she asked Jefri on the walk over? Before she could figure out what to do, Murat leaned forward and lightly kissed her cheek.

"Welcome, Ms. Van Horn. My brother complained of your great skill in the sky but he said nothing of your exceptional beauty."

She would have thought that older handsome prince set to inherit the kingdom would have had some effect on her when he'd kissed her. She'd braced herself for at least a toe curl, but there hadn't been even a flicker. Interesting. So her reaction was specifically to Jefri and not just to the whole good-looking-guy-in-the-palace thing. She would have to take that information out later and figure out what it meant.

"Most men don't enjoy being shot down by a woman," she said with a smile. "It's an ego thing. I don't take it personally."

"Billie is convinced I will not ever best her. I am going to have to prove her wrong."

Murat glanced between the two of them. "She does not look concerned, my brother. Perhaps you will have to content yourself with besting her in other ways."

The king entered the room, along with an obviously pregnant woman and what Billie took to be yet another of the handsome prince crop.

Jefri leaned close. "Perhaps my brother is right and I should seek other kinds of victories."

The combination of his words and his warm breath on her neck made her quiver.

"Come, you must meet our newest treasure," the king said, leading the couple toward them. "Billie, my son Reyhan and his beautiful wife Emma."

Billie had the whole purse/champagne thing under control this time. She'd tucked her bag under her arm so she was able to hold out her right hand to both of them.

"Welcome," Reyhan said pleasantly.

"Are you really a fighter pilot?" Emma asked.

"She is brilliant in the sky," Jefri said, answering for her.

"Amazing." Emma smiled. "I thought you would

be more…masculine. But you're lovely enough to be a pop star or an actress.''

Billie beamed. ''Aren't you sweet. I'm just a girl who likes to dress up. I tried being one of the boys for a long time and it never worked.''

''One cannot imagine why,'' Jefri murmured in her ear.

Murat returned with a scotch for his brother and a glass of what looked like sparkling water for Emma.

''What do you think of Billie?'' he asked. ''Is she not most intriguing?''

Jefri stepped between her and Murat. ''She is my guest.''

Billie felt a slight thrill. Was Jefri being possessive? Did he actually see her as something other than a means to fly better?

Another couple arrived—one of the princes accompanied by a petite, curvy blonde who squealed when she saw Billie.

''You're American. Yeah. We can hang out and talk while you're here. I'm Cleo. Hi. Do you realize that out of all four of the women who are in this family, I'm the only one who lives in the palace?'' She poked Emma's arm. ''You're constantly gone, as are Zara and Sabrina. It's really annoying.''

Cleo's escort, Prince Sadik, sighed. ''You have confused our guest and possibly frightened her.''

''Are you frightened?'' Cleo asked.

Billie laughed. ''No, just confused. What women? Who are Zara and Sabrina?''

''Perhaps we should adjourn to the table where we

can all straighten this out,'' the king said. ''Billie, you may sit next to me.''

So she found herself next to the king of Bahania, surrounded by honest to goodness princes and princesses. Billie had the fleeting thought that she wished her mother was still alive to take part in all this.

''All right, let me see if I have this right,'' she said over the soup course. ''Sabrina and Zara are princesses by birth.''

The king nodded.

''But Zara didn't know she was your daughter until about a year ago. And Cleo and Emma are Americans married to your sons.''

''That is correct.''

''Very complicated,'' she said as she discreetly moved the sliver of prosciutto she'd slipped off her appetizer plate into the Baggie.

''You will learn who belongs with whom,'' the king said kindly. ''Simply remember my sons favor American women.''

''Interesting point.''

She couldn't help glancing across the table to where Jefri sat. Did he favor American women as well? He seemed to be watching her, and while she wanted to believe it meant something, she'd been burned enough times to hold back. Ever since turning sixteen and having her first crush, she'd found herself interested in men who wanted nothing to do with her. It was like a curse.

''I have met one of your brothers,'' the king said. ''How many are there?''

"Three. I'm the only girl and the youngest."

"Sabrina could relate to that," Cleo said. "Her brothers made her life miserable. What about yours?"

"My mother always said they were a handful. She did her best to keep them in line."

"What does she think of your occupation?" Jefri asked.

"She died when I was eleven. I'm not sure she would have been thrilled with my hanging out with my brothers all the time, but she would have wanted me to be happy."

"Did your father remarry?" the king asked.

Billie shook her head. "We traveled a lot with the company. My mother had kept me home with her, but after she was gone, I went around the world, as well. It made for a very eclectic education." And nowhere to call home. But Billie had always known she would have to choose between her love of the sky and putting down roots.

Emma leaned toward her. "I would have thought someone raised by her father would have been more of a tomboy."

Billie laughed. "I tried being one for a while, but then I realized I made a lousy son, so I gave it up and surrendered to my inner girl."

"Hence the call sign?" Jefri asked.

She nodded.

He raised his glass. "To always surrendering to your inner girl."

If asked, Billie would have expected to explain that the royal family was stuffy and well, boring. But that

wasn't true at all. After grilling her about her life—
in the most pleasant way possible—they'd laughed
and talked and teased just like any other family she'd
met. Okay, the flatware had been gold, but the rest of
the meal had been surprisingly normal.

Whether it was the combination of too much champagne, the strange quarters or an evening spent getting
lost in Jefri's dark gaze, Billie found herself unable
to sleep. Giving up, she left Muffin snoring softly and
pulled on her robe, then walked into the living room
where she opened the French door leading to the balcony and stepped out into the quiet of the night.

A moon hung low in the sky and sent fingers of
light across the lapping sea. There were scents in the
air, smells she didn't recognize but knew would forever remind her of Bahania. The air was still, faintly
cool, but still pleasant.

"The good life," she said with a smile. "I doubt
anything is ever going to top this."

She leaned on the balcony and stared down at the
dark gardens. Slim shadows darted in and out of
bushes. Cats, she thought grimly. No doubt out to kill.
Why on earth would anyone think creatures like that
were pet-worthy?

"What has you so concerned?" Jefri said as he
came out of the darkness and moved next to her at
the railing. "You are frowning."

His unexpected appearance startled her, although
not enough to make her duck back inside. She had a
brief thought that she was in her nightgown, but then

reminded herself that she'd been a lot more uncovered in her evening gown.

"There," she said pointing toward the garden. "Cats."

He chuckled. "I will protect you from any who attempt to attack you." He glanced around. "Where is Muffin?"

"Sleeping. She needs her beauty sleep."

"Tell me she does not have one of those black sleep masks."

Billie laughed. "She doesn't."

"Good."

He leaned against the railing, his shoulder close to her own.

"Did you enjoy your evening with us?" he asked.

"Very much so." She glanced at him, taking in the dark slacks and the formal white shirt he'd unbuttoned. The tie was gone, as was the jacket, and he'd rolled his sleeves up to his elbows.

"I've never dined with royalty before," she said. "I thought I'd be more nervous but everyone made me feel very comfortable."

"I was concerned you thought there were too many questions."

"Not at all. I thought everyone was interested and genuine rather than grilling me."

"We are like other families?"

"Except for the prince thing."

"So you were impressed."

She smiled. "Not exactly."

He raised his eyebrows. "Why not?"

"Come on. How impressed could I be by wealth and a title when we both know I could blow you out of the sky in thirty-eight seconds?"

"Good point. However, I could impress you in other ways."

Oh, yeah, that was a serious possibility.

"I'm just the hired help," she said instead, and did her best to act casually. "In a few months, I'll be gone and you'll rule your own skies."

"Do you like that aspect of your job? Going from place to place?"

"Sometimes." She tucked her hair behind her ear. "I enjoy seeing the world, but sometimes I wouldn't mind having a permanent base of operations. The problem with that is I've yet to find a way to combine home and hearth with what I love to do."

"The flying."

"Exactly."

"How did you learn to fly?" he asked.

"My dad had always taken me up with him. I was handling single engine planes by the time I was ten. My mom tried to hold me back, which worked until she died. Then there was no one telling my dad no. I worked my way up to jets pretty quickly." She turned her head and smiled at him. "Having a mini air force in the family helped. What about you?"

"I have always loved flying. My father indulged me with lessons when I was twelve. I'm sure he thought it was something I would outgrow."

"But you didn't."

"You're right. The more I flew, the more I loved

it. I wanted to join an air force, but we did not have one here in Bahania and no other country would allow me to train. They did not want the responsibility of a king's son.''

"Huh. I never thought there would be discrimination against royalty.''

"You would be surprised.''

"Maybe, but don't expect any sympathy.''

"I am not.'' He turned so he faced her. "Your life has not been traditional.''

"I know. I'm glad for what I've experienced, but it hasn't come free. I'm going to be thirty in a few years. I'd like to get married and start on the whole baby thing, but I don't actually meet the kind of guys who would be interested in me.''

He frowned. "What are you talking about?''

"It's the whole blow up in the sky thing. Most men don't like it and compensate one of two ways. They get way too aggressive with me on the ground, or they ignore me. No one is ever just a guy.''

Although Jefri was making a good showing, she thought. If only he wasn't a real prince.

"You are not making any sense,'' he told her.

"Sense or not, what's what is. The men I work with don't see me as an available female.''

"Perhaps they are not willing to take on your brothers.''

Billie stared at him. "Excuse me?''

"Your brothers. Doyle warned me away from you this afternoon. After our flight.''

She heard the words, but she couldn't believe them. "He what?"

"The message was extremely clear."

"I... He..." She pressed her lips together and reached for a rational, coherent thought. "That lying, cheating, scummy pinhead," she muttered.

Was it possible? Were her brothers the reason no one ever asked her out?

She thought about how possessive they were of her. Of the things they said and how they worried about her.

"This is so like them," she said, feeling her temper rise. She couldn't believe it. She'd been date-free for years. How many guys had wanted to take her out only to be headed off by one of her brothers?

"I'm going to make them pay."

"I would request that you not make them suffer too much."

"Why?"

"Because they have kept other men away from you."

"Oh, right and that's a good thing, how?"

"You are still available to me."

Billie barely had time to process the sentence, which was probably for the best because the most eloquent thing she would have come up with was "Huh?" As Jefri spoke, he drew her into his arms and pressed his mouth to hers, so whatever else she was going to say faded into a soft, soul-stealing kiss.

He claimed her with a combination of passion and tenderness. Firm lips moved against her own, discovering, heating, delighting. Her temper faded as if it had never been, while liquid desire took its place.

She sighed and melted against him, letting her body lean against his and her arms rest on his strong shoulders. He smelled of cognac and night and mystery. He drew her closer still until they touched as intimately as their mouths. One of his hands tangled in her long hair while the other roamed over her back.

Instinctively she tilted her head, to make the kissing easier. He responded by brushing his tongue against her lower lip. Anticipation raced through her and she parted for him. But instead of deepening the kiss, he moved away. He kissed her cheek, then along her jaw. When he reached the sensitive skin below her ear, he licked that spot and made her shiver. He took her earlobe in his mouth and gently grated his teeth.

Fire raced through her. Her breasts swelled as her nipples puckered into tight sensitive points of need. She felt overdressed and jumpy, as if her skin was suddenly too tight. Heat settled between her legs. She wanted to rub against him, she wanted to touch and be touched, she wanted to beg.

He returned his mouth to hers. Again she parted for him, but he kept the kiss chaste, barely touching, moving back and forth. Need filled her, unfamiliar yet welcome. The wanting grew.

At last, when she thought she was going to have to scream or maybe throw herself off the balcony, he slipped his tongue inside her mouth and circled it against hers.

Yes, she thought, giving in to the exquisite sensations that filled her. Arousal shook her, making her need so much more than this kiss. Yet she didn't want the kiss to end. She wanted him dancing with her like this for always.

But it was not to be. Eventually he drew back and she knew it was important to act with dignity and not whimper. In the faint light from her room, his eyes glowed with a need that both thrilled and frightened her.

"You are a woman of many surprises," he said as he stroked her cheek.

"The same could be said of you. Not the woman part," she added, feeling more than a little foolish. "You're a man of surprises."

"Thank you."

He brushed his thumb across her mouth. "I look forward to what tomorrow brings," he said. "Sleep well."

"Good night."

She waited until he disappeared into the darkness before stepping into her room. Sleep well? With her body on fire and her mind swirling? Between the kiss and what he'd told her about her brothers, she wasn't sure she was ever going to sleep again. Which was fine. She could spend the night planning her revenge against all the Van Horn men.

Chapter Four

Jefri arrived for his weekly meeting with his father a few minutes early. The king's office was near his own. Several guards stood on duty, while dozens of staff members raced around with folders and stacks of papers.

The king's senior assistant waved Jefri in. One of the wide double doors stood open and several people filed out.

Jefri waited until they'd left before walking inside. He found his father standing behind his desk, flipping through a calendar.

"I'm thinking of visiting Europe," the king said without looking up. "With Murat taking over most of my state duties and the other work divided between you, Sadik and Reyhan, there is little to keep me here."

Jefri grinned. "Are you complaining you do not have enough to do?"

"I suppose I am. It is a sad state of affairs when a king is no longer needed."

Jefri took a seat on the visitor's side of the desk. "I think it is unlikely you will be beheaded anytime soon."

His father sat down and smiled. "How you comfort me." He leaned back in his chair. "So our new air force is off to a positive start?"

"Of course. The Van Horn team is in place. All the instructors have arrived. Billie is in charge of them."

The king nodded. "A most pleasant young woman."

Jefri could think of several words to describe Billie, but pleasant wasn't one of them. It was too bland, too lacking in style. Billie could never be accused of either.

"She assists in the pilot training, both with actual flying and in simulators. The Van Horn people have prepared an intensive eight-week program to forge our pilots into a team. When the initial instruction is finished, they will return to offer refresher courses until we get our own training in place."

"Very impressive," the king said. "I would advise you not to annoy her. I would hate to lose you because, to quote the young woman herself, she blows you out of the sky."

Jefri smiled. "I will not allow that to happen."

"It sounds as if she is unbeatable."

"Perhaps."

But he had a feeling he knew her weaknesses. Last night she had melted in his arms. Whatever her skills in the sky, on ground, she was mere woman. He planned to take advantage of that fact, pleasing them both along the way. He did not believe she could respond to him so easily in the night and then destroy him, however much in theory, during the day.

For now he only needed an edge to best her. In time, he would develop the skills to take her on his own.

"I am glad all goes well," his father said. "Now on to another matter. I have found you a bride."

Jefri almost asked "For what?" before he recalled a conversation with his father some months ago, when he had given in to parental pressure and agreed to remarry.

"Perhaps this is not the best time," he began.

"You are my son. It is your duty to produce heirs."

"I am but twenty-nine. There is still time."

"For you, perhaps," the king said. "But I do not grow younger. You asked me to find you an appropriate young woman." He pulled a sheet of paper out of a drawer. "You said she was to be docile, reasonably attractive and good with children. That is who I found."

Jefri wondered what he had been thinking when he had made that particular request. Yes, he had to marry, and an arranged match was as good as any, but now?

"I have other priorities at this moment. The air force takes much of my time."

"Your bride will require little of you," the king said. "You were specific when we spoke. You did not want this to be a love match."

That much was true, Jefri thought. He had already played at that game and lost. Love was not for him. Better to find someone who could do the job and not manipulate his heart. Respect was far more important than love.

Without wanting to, he remembered a woman in the moonlight. The feel of a soft feminine body in his arms and a passionate response to his kiss. Billie was a temptation, but she did not meet any of his criteria save one. While it was possible she enjoyed children, he doubted anyone would ever accuse her of being docile. Worse, describing her as "reasonably attractive" was as much of an understatement as saying the center of the sun was mildly warm.

"I do not wish to be engaged at this time," Jefri said firmly.

He had no intention of marrying Billie, but that did not mean he could not enjoy her company.

"Arrangements have been made," his father told him.

"Then they need to be unmade."

The king stared at him for a few seconds. Jefri braced himself for a battle of wills. While he might be victorious against his father, he had little success against the king.

At last the older man nodded. "As you wish."

"Thank you, Father." He glanced at his watch. "I am due at the airport shortly."

"Then you must go. Be sure to tell Billie how much I enjoyed her company last night." His father smiled. "Tell her that next time I will ask the staff to prepare a plate for her to take back to her dog. It is not necessary for her to slip food into her handbag."

So the king had noticed as well. Jefri grinned. "I look forward to passing along the message."

Billie knew that Doyle had been out until nearly four in the morning, overseeing the equipment unloading. In deference to his late bedtime, she waited until ten before entering his suite and stalking toward the bedroom.

Between the kiss and her fury at what she'd found out, she hadn't gotten much sleep herself, which meant she'd had plenty of time to work up a head of steam. A tiny part of her looked forward to exploding all over her brother.

As she'd expected he was asleep. She crossed to the windows and pulled open the drapes. As light spilled onto the bed, he stirred, then rolled onto his back.

"What the hell are you doing?" he growled. "Do you know what time I got to bed?"

"Ask me if I care," Billie said as she moved close to the side of the bed and glared down at her brother. "You are so in trouble. Don't for one second think you're going to talk your way out of this. I mean to have your head on a platter. Or maybe a stick. I haven't decided.''

Doyle stretched and yawned. He looked amazingly unconcerned as he sat up and leaned against the headboard. His sleep-mussed hair fell across his forehead and stubble darkened his jaw.

''You're sure flapping your lips,'' he said with a complete lack of concern for her temper. ''But you're not saying much.''

She picked up one of his boots and tossed it at him. ''Don't you dare dismiss me, you rat. How dare you run my life? You don't have the right.''

He batted away the flying boot and stared at her. ''You've gone over the edge.''

''Not yet, but I'm really close.'' She picked up the other boot and was pleased to see him duck. ''That's right. Be afraid. Because you have messed with something you're going to regret.''

''Put that down,'' he said, lunging toward her.

She was careful to keep out of reach, knowing she was safe as long as Doyle couldn't grab her. Like all her brothers, he slept in the nude, so he wasn't going to be getting out of bed anytime soon. She raised the boot again and glared.

''You've been warning men away from me, telling them who knows what so they won't ask me out. How dare you? What I want to know is what gives you the right? I've been an adult for a long time. I'm capable of making my own decisions.''

He winced. ''You're crazy.''

''Am I? I couldn't figure out why perfectly nice

guys who had been flirting with me suddenly showed no interest. I thought it was me. But it wasn't. It was you guys. And Dad. He's in on it, too, isn't he?''

''We just thought—''

''What?'' she demanded, threatening him with the boot. ''That I was too fragile to take care of myself.''

''After what happened before, we thought it was a good idea.''

Not a surprise, she told herself. ''Doyle, that was eight *years* ago. I'm not happy it happened, but didn't it occur to you that I'm over it?''

''What if some guy tries to hurt you again?''

''I'll deal with it. You can't protect me. It's wrong to try.'' She set down the boot. Figures, they'd done the wrong thing for the right reason. ''This stops right now. You get out of my personal life.''

He folded his arms over his chest. ''Or what?''

She stared at him, at the familiar square jaw and blond hair. At the powerful muscles. When she'd been little and the constant subject of their endless teasing, she always thought that when she got bigger she would be able to take them on. But she'd been wrong. They still thought of her as their baby sister. Someone who wasn't quite big enough or grown-up enough or good enough. It didn't matter that she could blow every one of them, including her father, out of sky in less than three minutes.

''If you all don't stop treating me like a child, I'm leaving the business.''

Doyle stared at her. ''You're bluffing. You love it too much to leave.''

She did love it, but she wouldn't stay somewhere she couldn't be her own person. "You know I get six job offers a month. I mean it, Doyle. I'll walk."

He swore under his breath, then held up his hands in a gesture of surrender. "Fine. I'll talk to Dad and the guys. It may take us a while to, you know, act differently."

"I'm sure you're more than up to the task."

He grumbled something under his breath, no doubt calling her names. None of her brothers had ever been especially gracious losers.

"I need to get to the airport," she said brightly. "I have simulation training this afternoon." She started to walk out of the room.

"Hey. What about the drapes," he yelled after her.

"Get up and close them yourself."

Feeling more than a little empowered, Billie walked back toward her rooms. She still had to collect Muffin before heading to the airport. In her own car with her own driver, she thought with a grin. Ah, it was good to be her right now.

She rounded a corner and nearly ran smack into Prince Jefri. All her breezy confidence drained away, leaving her feeling awkward, silly and tongue-tied.

"You appear to be very cheerful," he said as he stopped in front of her. "Is there a reason?"

Man, oh man did he look good, she thought as she took in the dark suit, pale blue shirt and striped tie. Princes had the best clothes and some really great tailoring.

"I, ah…" What was the question? Oh, yeah. "I just told my brother off."

"Did it go well?"

"Not bad. I believe he got the message."

A smile tugged at Jefri's mouth. "Did you threaten him?"

"Of course. Isn't that what sisters do?"

"I don't recall my sister threatening me much, but she spent much of the time in America. Was there blood spilt?"

"No, although I did throw his boot at him."

"Impressive."

She laughed. "He'd worked until early this morning. I think it's the only reason I got the drop on him, but I won't ever admit that to him."

"Of course not. Nor will I."

Awareness crackled between them. They'd kissed about twelve hours before and she was still experiencing aftershocks. Was Jefri? As a handsome prince was he used to kissing all sorts of women and had theirs been just one in a long line?

"What are you thinking?" he asked unexpectedly.

She felt her eyes widen. "Nothing important."

"I think it was very important." He moved closer. "Will you not tell me?"

"I just…" She cleared her throat. "It looks like another great day. Too bad we'll be doing simulations instead of flying for real."

His dark gaze settled on her face. "That was a rather poor and obvious attempt to change the subject."

"I know, but you're so well mannered, I figured you'd let me get away with it."

"Hmm, and here I had hoped you would tell me you had been busy thinking about last night." He lowered his voice. "I enjoyed our conversation and our kiss."

Holy moly. He was going to *talk* about it? She wasn't used to that, but then she wasn't much used to kisses from princes. Or men in general. Jeez, based on what she'd just found out about her brothers she should send every guy who *had* gathered the courage to ask her out an award of some kind.

"I had a nice time, too," she said primly.

He raised his eyebrows. "Nice? I see I must work on my technique."

Before she could respond, she felt something brush against her bare ankles. She looked down, then scrambled out of the way of a small calico cat.

"Those creatures are everywhere," she muttered.

Jefri bent over and picked up the cat. It wasn't much bigger than his hand and as he held it, the cat began to purr. Billie could hear the soft rumble.

"She likes you," he said.

"She's trying to lull me into a false sense of security before the attack."

He petted the cat. "I doubt she weighs more than five or six pounds. You do not appear to be in any imminent danger."

"So you say."

She watched as he scratched the feline under its

chin. It twisted around to get on its back and nearly fell off his hand.

"Careful," Jefri said, nestling the cat against his chest. "You are too trusting, I think."

"Especially around me," Billie said.

He looked at her. "You would not hurt a kitten."

"No, but I'd be happy to threaten it forcefully with words."

"But she has done you no harm."

"You keep saying *she*. It could be a boy."

"Unlikely. Calicos are generally female, much as marmalades are usually male. This one is maybe eight or nine weeks old."

The kitten rolled onto her back and splayed her paws as Jefri rubbed her tummy.

"Come now," he said. "Touch her fur. I suspect she is not nearly as horrible as you would have me believe."

Billie wrinkled her nose, but did as he requested. She touched the white fur under the cat's chin.

"Soft," she said in some surprise. She could feel the warmth of its body and the rumble from the purring.

The kitten blinked slowly, as if dozing off.

"She does seem to trust you," Billie said.

"I'm very good with females."

"Like that's a surprise."

He shifted the cat so it lay on its tummy, then handed it to her. Billie stepped back and shook her head.

"No, thanks. I'll admit she's kind of cute, but I'm

not interested. As far as I'm concerned, the entire cat population still has a lot to answer for.''

He set down the kitten and shook his head. ''You are a most difficult woman.''

''I know. It's part of my charm.''

Jefri stared down at the instrument panel. Everything was as it should be, but even doing everything correctly did not stop the high-pitched tone-lock he heard in his ears. He tore off the headset, hit the switch to kill the simulation and stepped out of the machine.

Again. She had done it again. At least in his first and second simulation he had lasted nearly three minutes. This time she had nailed him in less than forty seconds.

Annoyance grew to anger. He narrowed his gaze as he swept the room, finally locating Billie stepping out of her simulator. In her denim skirt and tight T-shirt, she looked more like a college coed than a fighter jet instructor. Long blond hair tumbled down her back. She wore impossibly high-heeled sandals. She was walking, breathing sexual desire incarnate and he was not sure if he should strangle her or push her up against the wall and have his way with her.

Wariness darkened her blue eyes. He saw a flash of something that might have been disappointment, then she squared her narrow shoulders, raised her chin and walked toward him.

He recognized her determination. She was prepared

to take him on—to endure his ill temper in the name of making him a better pilot.

"I know you're pissed off," she said as she approached. "You got too cocky in that last run and didn't think. You always have to respect your opponent because up there, the ordinance is real and you can get dead really fast."

Light spilled in from a window and illuminated her pale skin. Color stained her cheeks, but he suspected it came from her being upset rather than a cosmetic.

"You need to let go of the fact that I'm a woman," she told him, sounding delightfully earnest. "I have knowledge to share with you. That's it."

She continued to speak, expressing platitudes designed to restore a fragile male ego.

Of course, he told himself. This was her world. Every new client had pilots who resented her ability simply because she was a woman. How long had she been apologizing for being the best?

She was the most amazing woman. Bright, determined, talented. Erotically sensual.

He wanted her with every cell of his being, but even more than that, he wanted to make things all right for her.

"Meet me in an hour," he said, cutting her off in midsentence.

She blinked at him. "Excuse me?"

"Meet me in front of the Van Horn office in an hour." He glanced over her short skirt and tight T-shirt. "Bring a jacket."

"I have classes. I have other students who…"

He pressed a finger to her lips to still her words and to feel the warmth and softness of her skin.

"Please," he said. "I have something I want to show you."

Chapter Five

Billie walked to the front of the Van Horn office as Jefri had requested. She'd even brought along a jacket, although it had to be close to eighty degrees in the shade. Nothing in her previous work experience had prepared her for this kind of a situation and she was still figuring out how to deal with it when Jefri pulled up in an open Jeep and patted the passenger seat invitingly.

"I understand that you're the prince and everything," she said as she climbed inside, "but that's not important to the rest of my students. I have a responsibility to them as well as you and I can't disappear on a moment's notice just because you will it."

He grinned and drove through the airport. "Actually, you can. I promise not one of your students will complain."

"But that's because you're in charge of the air force."

"Yes."

Obviously she wasn't getting through. "You need to use your power for good, not evil."

His dark eyes crinkled at the corners. "I promise nothing evil will happen today."

"I'm not sure that's good enough."

"You will have to trust me."

Something she wasn't prepared to do. Not completely. He was the kind of man who hated being defeated by anyone and her ability to consistently cramp his winning streak was problematic. The thing was, she didn't know what to do about it. Usually she accepted the situation and moved on. But with Jefri...

If he'd been a lousy kisser none of this would have mattered. Or if he didn't make her heart beat so fast. If she didn't like him she wouldn't care that she had the potential to grind his ego into dust.

"Stop thinking," he told her. "You are here to enjoy yourself and be impressed."

"This isn't about flying, is it?" she asked. "That's kind of a bad place to try to impress me."

He smiled. "We shall see."

Maybe she could *pretend* to be impressed, she thought, as he circled behind the hangars for Bahanian Air and headed for a large, unmarked structure. If she could just act like other women, then she could coo and swoon and do all those girly things. Lord knows she had the hair products to go all gooey.

Jefri stopped by the door to the large structure.

"When you get out, I want you to cover your eyes."

She glanced at him. "Not exactly my style."

"Please. I want this to be a surprise."

And she wanted to see him smile again. "Okay."

She climbed down, then covered her eyes with one hand. He took the other and led her into the building. She immediately sensed the change from bright sunlight to dim shade.

"Do not move," he said, stepping away.

She heard footsteps, then a click, followed by an explosion of light.

"Now," he told her.

She opened her eyes and looked around. The gasp of appreciation didn't have to be faked. She meant it all the way down to her toes.

"You're kidding," she breathed as she took in a hangar full of beautiful restored old planes.

She spotted a Tiger Moth, a Fokker, even a Spitfire. Billie felt her chest getting tight as she tried to take in the wonders of Jefri's very private air museum.

"I can't believe it," she breathed. "You own these?"

"This is only part of my collection," he said as he walked toward the large airplane-sized hangar doors and pushed a button. The huge metal doors began to open.

"Several of my planes are at the Bahanian national museum. A few are taken around to air shows."

He walked over and took her hand, then led her to the Tiger Moth.

"Your headgear and goggles are there," he said pointing to a small table beside the plane.

Her mouth dropped open. "We're going up in it?"

"Of course." He grinned. "They are all fully functional."

"I... You..." Okay, so she was stunned past talking. Fine with her.

She circled the old plane and ran her hands lovingly along the fuselage.

"Amazing," she breathed.

"Here."

Jefri tossed her a leather helmet and goggles. She slipped into her jacket, then the helmet. The step up presented a bit of a problem. Billie judged the distance, the skimpiness of her skirt and her high-heeled sandals. There seemed to be only one solution.

She stepped out of her shoes and grabbed them in one hand. After tucking her goggles into her jacket pocket, she reached for the handholds and pulled herself up and into the plane. She had a feeling that she'd probably flashed Jefri along the way, but she was too happy to care.

"She's fabulous," she called as he took the position behind hers.

"She's my favorite," he admitted.

Two men in gray jumpsuits walked over and pulled the blocks away from the wheels. Jefri started the engine. As the plane slowly moved forward, Billie studied the simple design of the cockpit, the minimal information provided.

But what the plane lacked in technology it made

up for in sheer flying pleasure, she thought as they moved down the runway then eased off the ground. The Tiger Moth flew at a speed close to a jet's stall level. They were airborne, yet only a few dozen feet from the ground. There was no pull of G-force, no sense of power or thrust or barely controlled power.

Instead she could feel the rush of the air as they moved higher and faster. The more they climbed, the more the temperature dropped, making her glad for her jacket. The airport got smaller and smaller below, yet the sky seemed infinitely vast above them. In a jet, she had a sense of wanting to get there quickly. In the Tiger Moth, she wasn't sure she wanted to arrive at all.

"Here. You try it," Jefri yelled from behind her.

She took the stick and felt the old plane respond to her touch. She slowed down, then sped up to get a feel for the parameters before trying a few lazy circles and a steep climb.

"Admit it," he said loudly. "You're impressed."

She laughed. "Absolutely. I want one."

"They're not that hard to come by."

Perhaps not, but she lived her life out of a suitcase. Sometimes it was difficult enough to get a room with a bathtub. Billie wasn't sure how she would drag another plane along. Still…maybe it was worth looking into.

She swooped over the city. The view was different than it had been in her jet. Now there was time to study the various buildings and notice how the blocks were so square and tidy. She saw the clear demarcation line where civilization gave way to the emptiness of the desert.

"I think I gave up on small planes too soon," she said. "I couldn't wait to go faster and faster. Now I'm not sure why."

"These were real workhorses in their time," he told her. "Planes like these were used to map the desert. It was too dangerous to do on foot."

A different time, she thought. Simpler. "I would have liked that job," she said. "Now there isn't any unknown to fly into."

Of course she still would have been a woman in a man's world. Somehow she didn't think it would have been any easier back then.

"You would have been at great risk," he said over the wind.

"In what way?"

He laughed. "We were not so civilized back then. The harem was still filled with beautiful women. Had you flown into our desert, I suspect you would have been captured and presented to my great-grandfather as a prize."

"I'm not sure how I feel about that."

"It would have been a great honor."

"To be one of the crowd? No thanks." She did a large figure eight. "Is there still a harem?"

"That part of the palace still exists, but it has been empty since my grandfather's time."

"How disappointing for you."

Jefri laughed. "I do not need to hold my women captive to keep them at my side."

Hardly a newsflash, she thought. All he would have to do was crook his finger and the ladies would come running. She liked to think that she would be different and at least try to resist, but she knew she was wrong.

"Go north," he said. "About thirty miles."

She checked the compass and turned the plane to the correct heading. Below them several roads cut through the desert. She searched for signs of nomadic tribes but saw none. No doubt they preferred to stay farther away from the city.

A few minutes later Jefri had her turn east. Up ahead she saw a small oasis and what looked like a very rudimentary runway.

"She will do the work for you," he said. "Let her down easily."

Billie dropped lower and lower, aiming the nose toward the runway. At the last minute, she pulled up slightly so the plane landed on the rear wheels first. A cloud of dust rose up as they slowed, then finally stopped.

"Welcome to my private paradise," he said.

She took off her goggles. "Is it really yours?"

"I claimed it when I first flew here at age twelve. No one has disputed my ownership, so yes, it is mine."

Must be nice, she thought as she collected her shoes and stepped out of the cockpit.

"Wait," Jefri said as he jumped down first.

He stood just below her and held out his arms. Ah, the hardships her career forced upon her, she thought cheerfully as she surrendered to gravity and allowed Jefri to catch her against his hard body.

He held her a fraction of a second longer than necessary, not that she minded, before assisting her with her shoes. They left their jackets, helmets and goggles in the plane and walked toward the clusters of plants and trees at the edge of the water.

"Are there underground springs?" she asked.

"Hundreds. My brother, Reyhan, has a house in the middle of the desert that sits on top of a spring. He and his wife live there now. The fabled City of Thieves is said to exist at the edge of an underground river."

Billie frowned. "I remember reading about the City of Thieves when I was doing research on your country. It is supposed to be hidden somehow. The way the buildings blend in with the land or something. One account I read said there was a medieval castle there."

"How interesting," Jefri said in a carefully neutral tone.

"Is it real? The city?"

He drew her close and brought her hand up to rest on his arm. "Bahania is a land of much beauty and many mysteries. Perhaps you should give yourself time to discover them all."

"Hardly an answer," she grumbled but without much energy. When faced with the beauty of the oasis, what did a mythical city matter?

He pointed out different types of trees and shrubs. She bent down to feel the softness of the grass that grew right to the edge of the large pond in the center of the oasis. The water lapped against the bank, as if driven by a tidal force.

"Why does it move like that?" she asked.

"The pressure of the feeding spring."

"Okay, so if the pond is being constantly fed with fresh water, why doesn't it overflow? It's not evaporating that quickly and I don't see any kind of drainage."

He smiled. "Yet another mystery to be solved. Things are more complex than they first appear."

He led her around a grove of palm trees where she saw two lounge chairs set up with a small table between. A cooler sat on the ground with a basket of fruit on top.

"You're kidding," she said with a laugh. "You planned this?"

"Down to the last detail. We'll be having lunch later."

"I know it's not in our plane, so did you have someone specially bring all this here?"

"Of course."

He spoke so casually, she thought as he led her to one of the lounge chairs. Talk about the thrill of royalty. She was lucky if she could convince one of her brothers to bring her back gum from the convenience store.

She settled down while he popped open the cooler. There were an assortment of cold sodas, juices and bottled waters. She liked that he wasn't going to drink while they still had to fly back.

When they were stretched out on their chairs and

sipping their drinks, she glanced around at the beauty and quiet of the desert.

"Did you run off here when you got in trouble as a kid?" she asked.

"Sometimes. My father learned fairly quickly that I could be kept in line with the threat of losing access to my planes."

"I know what you mean. In my house, getting grounded was meant literally."

He chuckled. "I doubt you received many lectures on your duties to the people and how when you got in trouble you were letting down a thousand years of tradition."

"Okay, I was spared that." She looked at him. "Did the king really bring up a thousand years of tradition in his lectures?"

"It was a particular favorite." Jefri shrugged. "According to him, I deeply disappointed all of our ancestors on a regular basis."

She couldn't imagine having that much history in one family. She got excited when she was able to stay in one place more than eight weeks.

"But you recovered to transgress another day," she said.

"Sometimes I did not wait that long." He smiled. "I liked to explore and I rarely followed the rules."

"Something tells me you still don't."

Instead of answering, he reached for her hand and took it in his. "Tell me what it was like when you were growing up. There was no king to make pronouncements."

"Maybe not, but my dad was used to being in charge. With three boys to deal with, he had to be firm."

Jefri rubbed his thumb across the back of her hand and made her skin tingle. "What about with you?"

"Until my mom died, she took care of disciplining me. I spent most of my time with her and we always got along. She used to say how as there were only two of us, we had to band together."

She felt his gaze on her face. "You must have found her death very difficult."

"I did. I was just about to enter the whole teenaged thing, when a girl really needs her mom. She had cancer, so there was some warning, but only a few weeks. By the time she realized she was sick, it was already too late. My folks had first started dating in high school and my mom once admitted they'd both been each other's first time. So when she got sick, my dad really freaked out."

She stared out at the horizon. "My dad traveled a lot and I thought that meant he didn't care so much about her, but I was wrong. I remember a couple of days after she'd been diagnosed and they'd told us, I went into their bedroom to talk to her. He was there, holding her. Crying. I'd never seen my dad cry. I didn't want to spy, but I couldn't seem to walk away. He begged her not to die. He told her he couldn't make it without her. I could feel their love for each other. I vowed then I would find someone to love me that much."

"Have you?" he asked.

She raised her eyebrows. "We wouldn't be sitting here holding hands if I had."

"An excellent point."

Funny how she'd begun to believe she *wouldn't* find anyone to love her that much because no one seemed to be interested in her. Knowing that her brothers were scaring off potential boyfriends made her feel a little better. Although did she want someone who didn't want her enough to go up against her brothers?

Too confusing, she told herself, and not something to be resolved today.

"So when your mother died, you went on the road with your father?" Jefri asked.

She nodded. "He'd started taking the boys with him during the summer. Now, with no one left at home, we all went. Dad hired a tutor so we could keep up with school. I turned thirteen in South America and sixteen in the Middle East. Most girls get a sweet sixteen party—I soloed on a jet."

"Would you rather have had the party?"

She looked at him and raised her eyebrows. "Are you crazy? I'd *begged* my dad to let me fly jets for two years before he let me. He said I couldn't handle the technical information, so I studied physics and aerodynamics until he was forced to change his mind."

Jefri watched the emotions move across Billie's face as she spoke. She was a beautiful woman, but it was not difficult to imagine the frightened young girl she must have been when she had lost her mother.

Frightened and alone, yet determined. What had *he* fought for when he had turned sixteen? As the youngest son of the king, he had been given nearly everything he wanted. If he recalled correctly his sixteenth birthday had involved a large party and a concert by a young female pop star.

"You survive in a very male world," he said.

She laughed. "At first it sucked me in. After my mom died I thought the only way to get along with my father was to be one of the guys. I thought that would make him respect me. Over time I finally figured out I would never be another one of his sons so I stopped trying."

"I cannot tell you how relieved I am."

She laughed. "No desire to date Doyle, huh?"

"None in the least."

"Around my nineteenth birthday, I said the hell with it. We were in France, at the air show. I spent two days getting my hair done, painting my nails and shopping. I went from combat boots to four-inch heels and I never looked back."

"What did they say?" he asked.

"No one even noticed for a while. My dad said he thought my skirts were too short and my brothers ragged on me for my big hair. I challenged them all to a simulated dogfight. It was the first time I beat them and I've been kicking their butts ever since."

"The power of a woman," he said, delighted by her victory.

"Something like that." She sipped her drink. "Don't get me wrong. I love my family. They're weird, but I think every family is. We live a very nomadic existence and that has made us appreciate the times when we are together.''

''Your father never remarried?''

''No. I wish he would. I know he loved my mom, but that's no reason for him to be alone for so long. I don't think she would have wanted it that way.'' She looked at him. ''Your father never remarried after your mother's death.''

''That's true. Theirs was a love match as well, although he'd been married before. I think he found raising four sons and a daughter took too much time. However my father takes long trips to Europe and America where I doubt he lacks for female companionship.''

''Good point. I doubt anyone is going to tell him she's not interested.''

He raised his eyebrows. ''Is that why you are with me? Because I am a prince and you do not think you can say no?''

She studied him from under lowered lashes. ''Pretty much.''

He saw the corner of her mouth quiver.

''I can see you are trying not to laugh,'' he told her.

''You're right, but if you could have seen your face when I said that. You believed me and you were deeply insulted.''

He released her hand and swung his legs to the ground. ''I can see I am going to have to teach you more respect for my lofty position.''

"I respect you, Jefri, but it's not as if I'm scared of you."

"Good to know. Are you ready for lunch?"

"Sure."

Billie's idea of al fresco dining involved take-out or a sub sandwich made under questionable circumstances with ingredients she didn't want to identify. But outdoor dining prince-style took on a whole new meaning. Not only was there a real wood table with matching chairs, a white linen tablecloth provided a perfect backdrop for elegant china and crystal.

A servant in a white jacket and black slacks materialized as they walked toward the beautifully set table. He held out Billie's chair and offered her a hand-printed menu of the various available selections. She looked over the many salads and entrées—not a sandwich in the bunch—then set down her menu and leaned toward Jefri.

"You're working very hard to impress me," she said.

"You told me that was not possible."

"I might have lied."

"Good."

He brushed her mouth with his and sent heat racing to all parts of her body.

"But remember," he said quietly. "These are only things and scenarios. They say nothing about who I am."

She knew what he meant. That he was more than a rich guy with hot and cold running servants. But he was wrong about his world not being part of who he was. Jefri wielded power as casually as most people drove a car. He commanded an impressive air force with enough firepower to destroy nearly any country on the planet and her job was to teach him to do that better.

"You're not exactly how I pictured a prince would be," she said.

"Is the impression better or worse."

"Different. But then I don't have a lot of experience in the royal world."

"Then we are even because I have little experience with delightful, sexy female flight instructors. Mine were always men. I would say it was my loss."

She smiled. "Absolutely."

He picked up her menu and handed it to her. "What would you like?"

"I'm not going to ask what's good. I'm assuming it's all fabulous."

"Of course it is. Oh, and if you're thinking of choosing something because you want to take the left-overs to Muffin, the king asked me to tell you to simply ask for a plate to be sent to your rooms. There is no need for you to slip food into your handbag."

She squeezed her eyes shut and held in a groan. "Did everyone notice I'd done that at dinner?"

"Of course."

She opened her eyes and stared at him. "I'm humiliated."

"You're charming. We were all entranced."

"I had a Baggie," she said, knowing it was a pretty

feeble explanation. "It's not like I put meat directly into my purse or anything."

"Of course not."

"So you don't think it's odd?"

He smiled. "I think it is extremely odd."

"You're mocking me."

"Absolutely."

Billie's pleasure in her oasis lunch with Jefri lasted exactly twenty-five hours and forty-two minutes, right until she found herself once again flying with him. But instead of sharing a beautifully restored Tiger Moth, they were flying separate jets and she was coming around for another pass.

What she hated was how quickly she was going to kill him. If only he'd lasted four or five minutes, they could both feel better about the experience. But the specially designed timer that was part of the training program had yet to hit ninety seconds and she already had him in her sights.

For a brief flicker in time, she thought about pretending that she couldn't get him, but as the thought formed, she pushed it away. Her job was to make her students into the best pilots possible and that wasn't going to happen by letting them win. She maneuvered until she was able to get a clear shot, then pushed the button. The sharp sound of tone-lock filled her cockpit and his sharp inhale of disbelief filled her headset.

"You continue to surprise me," he said.

"That's why they pay me the big bucks."

She couldn't tell what he was thinking from the

tone of his voice and she wasn't sure she wanted to know. She followed him down from the sky and landed. When she'd pulled her jet up to his, she hesitated before climbing down.

What was she going to say? How could she explain that it didn't matter to her that he didn't beat her in the sky? She still liked being around him, talking to him, flying with him, and she wouldn't object if he wanted to kiss her again.

"Sitting here is getting nothing done," she told herself and popped the canopy on her jet, then pulled off her helmet and climbed down.

As she crossed the tarmac, she saw Doyle walking toward Jefri. Something in her stomach warned her this could be trouble, so she hurried to catch up.

But she was too late and by the time she joined them she was just in time to see her brother slap Jefri on the back and hear him say, "It's gotta kill you to keep getting beaten by a girl."

"You get beaten by me all the time," she reminded her brother, wishing he could keep his mouth shut.

Doyle grinned. "Yeah, but I'm not a prince."

She wanted to scream in frustration. Instead she simply clenched her teeth and walked off. She didn't want to know what Jefri was thinking so she kept her gaze straight ahead as she made it back to the main tent. There she collected her street clothes and stepped into a restroom where she changed back into shorts and a T-shirt before stowing her gear and collecting Muffin.

"The entire situation makes me crazy," she told

her dog. "How am I supposed to win at this? I can't help being good and I don't want to change it."

She stepped out into the afternoon sun and nearly plowed into Jefri.

"What?" she demanded.

"I was looking for you."

"Okay. Fine. But here's the thing. I won't apologize for what I do well. I'm sorry if you're having ego problems."

"I do not consider my ego your responsibility."

He spoke quietly, even reasonably. That made her nervous. "I'm just doing my job," she continued. "Even though I know what they say. That I'm a ballbuster. It's not my plan to emasculate you, it just happens."

He grabbed her arms and led her around to the side of the tent, next to a stack of large crates.

"You talk too much," he said, his gaze intent on her face.

"I'm trying to explain."

"I understand perfectly. Put down that damn dog."

She was so surprised by the instruction that she did as he said. Then she was really glad when he pulled her close, wrapped his arms around her and kissed her.

The warm, insistent pressure against her lips made her cling to him. Heat flared, melting away all her concerns about him being upset or angry or anything the least bit negative.

His mouth moved slowly, as if giving her time to get used to what he was doing. If she'd been able to communicate without her mouth, she would have told him that she didn't mind the kissing at all. In fact, she really, really liked it. He could do more. Really.

Instead she placed her hands on his shoulders and let her body lean into his. She tilted her head and parted her lips in invitation.

He reacted with a sharp intake of air and a gentle sweep of his tongue against hers.

The kiss was as spectacular as it had been the first time. She felt her insides quiver, her knees shake and her thighs tremble. Heat poured through her, making her want and need with an intensity that stunned her.

One of his hands tangled in her hair, the other traced a line down her back until it settled on her rear. When he squeezed the curves, she arched forward, bringing her belly in contact with him.

Now it was her turn to gasp as she felt his arousal. He wanted her. After everything that had happened and what her brother had said, Jefri wanted her. Delight blended with desire and she nearly laughed.

He broke the kiss. "What do you find so amusing?" he asked, his breath mingling with hers.

"Just all of this."

"That I want to kiss you?"

"It is a bit of a surprise."

He cupped her chin and stared into her eyes. "Why? You're a beautiful woman. Unique, intelligent, desirable. I doubt there is a man alive who wouldn't sell his soul for one night with you."

She blinked at him. Whoa—talk about a great line. Right now she didn't even care if he meant it.

"I, um, thanks."

"You're welcome." He smiled as he rubbed his thumb against her lower lip. "I would very much like to have dinner with you tonight."

At this point in time, she would have followed him to the moon. "Okay. I mean, that would be great."

"Good. I'll pick you up at your room at seven. Is that convenient?"

As she'd planned to spend the rest of the afternoon soaking and grooming, seven sounded good.

"I'll be ready."

"We'll be going out," he said. "There are several excellent restaurants in the city. Will you allow me to choose?"

"Of course."

"Then it is a date." He dropped a brief kiss on her lips, then stepped back. "Leave the dog at home."

Chapter Six

Billie stood in front of her closet and reviewed her array of clothes. She believed in shopping, both as a sport and a way to relax, so there were plenty of outfits to choose from. She already knew she wanted something both sexy and sophisticated, with a touch of elegance thrown in. Which pretty much left out anything with feathers, rhinestones or too much beading.

She tilted her head, then straightened quickly as the curlers started to loosen. Tonight required perfect hair, which meant an hour spent in electric curlers and a double dose of hair spray.

"Everyone looks good in black," she murmured as she pulled out a clinging black dress with a deep vee and see-through sleeves. "But it's so predictable."

Maybe she should try a color. Not red. Somehow that just made her look trashy.

"Maybe blue," she said as she reached for a midnight-blue dress that had cost her nearly a month's salary in Paris.

The hand-painted bias-cut skirt fluttered just above her knees. The sleeveless bodice wasn't that low cut because the appeal lay elsewhere. From the waist up, the fabric was completely sheer. However the same hand-painted pattern that graced the hem of the skirt swirled across her breasts and the built-in bra in such a way that everything was perfectly covered. Yet there was the *promise* of being naked!

"This one," she said, carrying the dress into the bathroom. She had a perfect pair of high-heeled strappy sandals that made her ankles look as slender as swizzle sticks and some really high-end fake jewelry.

Billie had to admit her excitement about the evening was about more than just the whole "dine with a prince" thrill. Part of her was really happy that Jefri wanted to see her after his defeat earlier. That had never happened before and it gave her hope for his entire gender. While she believed her brothers had a part in warning men off, she couldn't help but think there had to be one or two willing to deal with their potential wrath unless their bruised egos had put them out of the mood.

A knock at the door made her panic. She glanced at the clock, but it was way too early for Jefri.

"Who is it?" she called from the center of the living room.

"Doyle."

She walked to the door and opened it. "Make it snappy," she said. "I'm busy."

He pushed past her into the room, then looked her over. "You don't look busy to me. You look like you're not doing much of anything. I need your help with some of the equipment."

"Not my area of expertise."

"Billie, I'm serious. The mechanics want to talk to you about one of the engines they're tuning. You know how you can tell what's wrong from the sound."

"Yes, it's a gift and one we can all take advantage of tomorrow. Now get out of here."

She pushed on her brother, but as he was about ten inches taller and oh, sixty pounds of muscle heavier, he didn't budge.

"What's your problem?" he demanded.

"I told you. I'm busy."

Doyle folded his arms over his chest and raised his eyebrows. "With what?"

She planted her hands on her hips and did her best to look stern.

"I have a date."

His expression hardened. "With whom?"

She knew he was mad whenever he started using really correct grammar. "I'm over twenty-one and you don't own me, so I don't have to say."

"I'm not leaving until you give me all the particulars."

She laughed. "Doyle, this isn't the nineteenth century. There aren't any particulars. A man asked me to dinner and I said yes. Get over it."

"You have a responsibility to this company."

"Oh, please." She rolled her eyes. "How many times have I covered for you? A thousand? I would say I'm entitled to a night off when I want it."

His gaze narrowed as he studied her. "It's that damn prince, isn't it?"

"I'm not sure you want to swear in front of his title. They might string you up for that."

He swore again. "Billie, I know you're mad about what we've all been doing."

"What? Oh, you mean running my life and warning off men behind my back?" She wanted to punch him but she knew that not only would she fail to really hurt him, she might mess up her freshly manicured nails.

"You were a pig," she told him instead. "All of you. You had no right and I deeply resent it."

"Fine. Be mad. Go out, but not with him."

"What's wrong with Jefri?"

"Nothing, except he's a damn prince."

"I actually know that."

He dropped his arms to his sides. "Billie, you're out of your league with a man like him."

She knew what he meant. That she was just the hired help and Jefri was royal.

"I'm not expecting anything more than dinner,

Doyle. You don't have to get your panties in a bunch.''

His mouth twisted. ''I don't wear panties.''

''I know, but you get my drift. You're making too much of this. It's just dinner.''

''Uh-huh. That's why you're spending five hours primping.''

''I haven't spent five hours.'' It had barely been two. ''Besides, grooming is fun.''

''You're not good at this kind of thing,'' he said. ''You don't have the practice.''

''Oh, right. And who's fault would that be? Hmmm. Yours?''

''Fine. Blame me. But at least start on someone easier. A regular guy. I could set you up with someone.''

''No, thanks. I'm not interested in who you think is right for me.''

She shuddered to imagine what kind of man Doyle would send her way. Someone bland, sexless and terrified of her brothers, most likely.

''He's completely wrong for you,'' Doyle told her.

''Maybe, but he asked me out to dinner and I said yes. I suggest you get over it.'' She walked to the door and held it open. ''I have to get dressed now.''

He walked toward the door, then paused. ''You're making a mistake, sis. He could crush you like a bug.''

As she knew he was genuinely worried, she decided not to kill him. ''I appreciate the concern, but I need to do this. Maybe I'm jumping into the deep end, but I'm a big girl. I know how to swim."

"Swimming won't help if he's a shark."

With that cheerful statement, Doyle walked out and she slammed the door behind him.

"Men," she muttered.

"The city planners wanted more than a typical high-rise skyline in the financial district," Jefri said as their car turned down the main boulevard. "While the buildings are tall, there are levels with gardens and art museums."

Billie leaned toward the window. "Is that one hollow?"

He chuckled. "Parts of it are. There is also an illusion of seeing through to the other side. That is part of the design."

"They're beautiful," she breathed as she turned her head to take in all the gleaming, modern structures.

"In the late 1970s my father realized that Bahania would not always be able to count on our oil reserves. That in three or four generations, the wells would begin to run dry and it was necessary for him to prepare his country for that future. In concert with the king of El Bahar, our neighbor, he opened trade markets and made financial institutions welcome."

She turned back to him and smiled. "That's some family history."

The sun had long set, leaving the city bathed in the glow of streetlights. The illumination barely penetrated the limo, so he couldn't see much more than her profile and a hint of her features. Still, her beauty took his breath away. Talking about the changes in the city over the past thirty or forty years might not be interesting, but he knew the information by heart and didn't have to consider his words. Were they to discuss something more personal, he had a feeling he might verbally stumble.

She stunned him. That the confident, capable woman who flew as if she'd been born to the sky could also look like a goddess seemed impossible. Yet it was true.

She shifted slightly on the leather seat and her hair caught the light. Soft curls cascaded down her back. A few tendrils teased her ears and her neck, although she'd piled most of her hair up on her head. Her dark blue eyes seemed to glow with feminine secrets. And that dress. He swallowed hard and did his best not to notice the transparent fabric and the way only a few brushstrokes of color and paint concealed her curves from view.

He would not be able to eat, he thought grimly. How on earth could he sit across from her in a public place and act as if nothing was wrong? He was Prince Jefri of Bahania, yet with Billie he was little more than a man humbled by a woman.

"What are you thinking?" she asked. "If you were some kind of wild animal I would swear you were stalking dinner."

"You are not far wrong," he said and lightly touched her bare arm. "You are most desirable prey."

She shivered, but didn't look away. Long lashes shielded her eyes. Earrings glittered and dangled.

"Have I told you how beautiful you are?" he asked in an attempt to keep from claiming her right there in the car.

"You mentioned it a couple of times, but it's not a topic of conversation that's going to bore me." She smiled. "It's not the sort of thing I hear that often."

"Then the men you know are blind fools."

"You got that right." She laughed. "And I appreciate how kind you're being. I'm just part of the staff and you're going out of your way to make me feel like a princess. I know you usually date movie stars and heiresses."

Kind? She thought he was being *kind?*

Before he could tell her that he had no kindness in mind, they pulled up in front of the restaurant. Billie leaned toward his side, the curbside.

"Wow. Look at all those people. Is there something going on here?"

Jefri followed her gaze, then swore.

"What?" she asked. "Is there a problem?"

"Not one that can be fixed. I am sorry. I did not think to tell my assistant to make reservations in another name. I am sure he did not think of it either."

She was close enough that he could feel the heat of her body and inhale the sweetness of her perfume. Both were a temptation.

"I don't understand," she said, apparently oblivious of her amazing charms.

"These people are with the press."

"Really?" She leaned past him to look at them through the window. Several had crowded around the limo. "Who are they waiting for?"

"Us."

She straightened and stared at him. "What? Oh. Right. You're the prince." She clutched her impossibly small purse to her chest. "I'm going to be something of a disappointment."

He shook his head. "Somehow I doubt that."

Billie's lack of awareness delighted him. Not only had she been unaware of why the press were there, she seemed blind to her own appeal. So many women he took out were secretly thrilled to be photographed for tabloids.

"So what happens?" Billie asked. "Do you go on ahead and then I sneak in through the back?"

He stiffened. "You are with me. We will walk in together."

She eyed the jostling crowd. "This really isn't my kind of thing. I hope I don't trip."

"Would you prefer to return to the palace?"

She hesitated, then glanced down at her dress. "I did sort of go to a lot of trouble to get all fancy. Will it be crazy inside?"

"No. The photographers won't be allowed in the restaurant. We'll be shown to a private table where we will dine just like any other patron."

He could see her weighing the possibilities.

"You decide," she said. "Let's do what you want."

Not a possibility, he thought, as his wants and desires had very little to do with dining in a restaurant.

"The food here is excellent," he said, as he nodded at the driver. "You will enjoy it. We will even order a special entrée for Muffin."

Billie tried to focus on food and her dog as the rear door of the limo opened and Jefri stepped out. The explosion of flashbulbs caught her unaware and temporarily blinded her. She slid along the leather seat until she could step out in front of the restaurant. A second barrage of bright lights left her totally unable to see.

Someone took her hand. She knew instantly it was Jefri and she allowed him to lead her toward the restaurant. She had a sense of the crowd pressing close. People called out questions, but she couldn't discern one voice from another.

Stay calm, she told herself. Think happy thoughts. She didn't want to see herself with a "deer in the headlights" expression on the front of some supermarket tabloid.

They made their way into the restaurant with only a few more flashes in her face. Once inside, the elegant and quiet atmosphere instantly calmed her.

"Prince Jefri," the maître d' said with a smile. "Thank you for dining with us this evening. We have your table ready."

Jefri nodded for her to follow the man. She leaned close and whispered, "What? They're not going to put our names on a sheet of paper and then call out when our table is ready?"

He raised his eyebrows. "Restaurants do that?"

She grinned. "You need to get out more."

He chuckled and took her hand.

Billie liked the way he laced his fingers with hers as they walked into the dining room. They wove through the well-dressed patrons seated at beautifully set tables. The smell of the food made her mouth water.

"Will this be acceptable?" the man asked.

"It's fine—" Jefri started before Billie interrupted with a soft shriek.

She stared at the table next to the empty one where the maître d' held out a chair.

"You're not here," she said, both furious and humiliated.

Doyle picked up his glass of wine in a salute. "Hey, kid. You should try the house salad. It's really good and you know I'm not much of a salad guy."

She couldn't believe it. Her brother? Here?

"You have no right to do this," she told him, careful to keep her voice low.

"Is there a problem?" Jefri asked.

"Yes. Him." Billie pointed at Doyle and wished she could incinerate him with her gaze. "He's spying on us."

"She's right," Doyle said, sounding amazingly cheerful. "I called your assistant and asked where you two were having dinner." He put down his wine. "Just so you don't behead him or anything, I told him my sister had asked me to check because she has food allergies and wanted to make sure there was something she could eat.''

Fury filled her, making her mad enough to spit. ''I do *not* have food allergies.''

''I know.'' He grinned. ''I was being creative.'' He motioned to their table. ''You two should have a seat. The food here is great and the wine list is impressive.'' He winked at Jefri. ''You probably know all this, don't you? You come here a lot.''

Billie glanced from her brother's table to Jefri's. They were barely two feet apart. Doyle would hear everything she said, which was probably his point. While intellectually she understood he was trying to protect her, emotionally, she was outraged.

''We could ask them for a different table,'' Jefri said. ''Or would you prefer to leave?''

Billie thought of how the patrons would be watching them through the entire meal and how she would be aware of Doyle sitting so close.

She sighed. ''I'd rather go back to the palace.''

Doyle's gaze narrowed. ''Billie—''

She cut him off with a shake of her head. ''Stay out of it. You've already done enough.''

''You know why.''

''That doesn't excuse it. I'm all grown-up, Doyle. It's time to let go.''

An hour later Billie and Jefri sat on the floor of her suite, leaning against the sofa and looking over the leftovers brought up from the king's formal dinner the previous evening.

"Better?" he asked as he poured her a glass of wine.

Billie stretched out her bare legs and wiggled her toes. Okay, even though the dress had been great, she was far more comfortable in shorts and a T-shirt.

"Much. Although my hair and makeup is a little overdone for the setting."

Jefri, who had also changed into more casual clothing, looked her over. "I would say you're exactly right."

She grinned. "You do have a way with words. Do princes have special classes in that sort of thing? Charming women and dealing with annoying photographers?"

"We are taught many skills. Being charming is one of them."

"You're not all that," she said.

He leaned close and smiled. "Too late. You have already admitted to being impressed."

"Maybe." She grabbed a shrimp and dipped it in the sauce. "So does the press usually follow you around?"

"Not as much as they used to. I would guess that you were the attraction tonight."

"Hardly. Why would they care about me?"

"They would be interested in *my* latest interest."

"Ah." Is that what she was? His interest? Was that like dating? She desperately wanted to know but was afraid to ask.

"When I was younger, the press trailed me everywhere," he said. "My father was able to exert some control here, but when I was in Europe or America, things could be difficult. We were given peace only when we were at school.''

"Must be tough being so popular.''

"There are compensations.''

"Sure. Like access to any available female you want. Kind of makes you wish there was still a working harem in this place.''

He picked up his glass of wine. "You exaggerate my reputation.''

"I don't think so. Are you telling me anyone has ever said no?''

She happened to be looking at him as she asked the question. For a split second something dark flashed through his eyes. Then he smiled.

"I would never tell you that,'' he said.

Interesting, she thought. Something from his past. She might have to do some checking on the Internet and find out if there had been a woman Jefri had cared about. She couldn't imagine anyone leaving him, though. Not just because he was a prince, but because he was a great guy and someone any woman would enjoy being with.

"What about you?'' he asked. "What are your romantic secrets?''

Billie froze in the act of offering a piece of chicken to Muffin. Her Yorkie took matters into her own paws and jumped up to grab the morsel.

"Secrets?'' Billie asked, hoping she sounded casual rather than nervous and faintly foolish. "I don't have that many.''

Jefri's dark eyes seemed to see into her soul. "You must have some. While I applaud your brother's concern, I believe it stems from more than fraternal worry. I think there is a reason he keeps such close watch on you."

"I... You can't know that."

Jefri shrugged. "We were to dine in a very public restaurant tonight yet Doyle felt it necessary to be there to watch over you. Why is he so afraid for your safety?"

She debated telling him the truth for all of eight seconds, then sighed.

"I had a couple of bad experiences when I was younger," she admitted without looking at him. "When I was nineteen, I went out with a group of pilots we were training. It was the first time one of my brothers hadn't tagged along. Everybody drank too much, except me. Even though I was above the drinking age, I hadn't developed a taste for anything really alcoholic. Even now I really only like wine, so I barely ever even get very tipsy."

He touched her bare leg. "Billie, as entertaining as I find your stories, perhaps tonight you could stay on topic."

That was easy for him to say. He didn't know what the topic was. She reminded herself that she was nearly ten years older and wiser. She'd learned to handle herself and to not put herself into those kind of situations anymore.

"Okay. Sure." She wiggled her shoulders in an effort to relax. "Well, you can imagine. Five guys, me and a lot of liquor. They got too friendly and when I tried to stop them, it didn't go well. Two of the guys dragged me back to the van and tried to…well, you know.''

She felt him stiffen. Rage tightened the muscles of his face and his expression became frighteningly determined.

''They didn't rape me,'' she said quickly. ''Doyle and Xander drove up before they'd done much more than scare the crap out of me. The guys took off and my brothers brought me back to the base.''

Jefri wondered how much she did *not* say. There was more to a rape than actual penetration. Had they hurt her? Marked her? Bruised more than her body?

He looked at her delicate features, her pale skin and the trust in her blue eyes. Fury filled him until he wanted to destroy those who had dared to attack her in such a way.

He swore, even as he struggled for control. ''What was done to them?'' he demanded.

''My brothers pounded them into quivering bloody masses, then they were kicked out of the program.''

He felt some small measure of satisfaction at that. But it was not enough. ''They should have been thrown into prison.''

''I know. I wanted to press charges, but we were in a foreign country and the laws were different.'' She shook her head. ''It's okay. I'm better now.''

He touched her cheek. ''You should not have anything to get better from. Tell me their names. I will bring them here and visit Bahanian justice upon them.''

''Which involves what?''

''Prison. Beating. Perhaps death.'' He liked the idea of them dead.

Her eyes widened. ''Death?''

''No man has the right to defile any woman. Ever. It has been that way here for nearly three hundred years.''

''A really good reason to take up residence,'' she murmured. ''Look, I appreciate your concern. Really. It's very sweet of you to worry, but I'm okay. It was nine years ago. I'm over it.''

He heard the words but did not believe them. He read a fragility in her eyes that told him those ghosts still had the power to haunt her.

''I see now why your brothers are so protective of you,'' he said.

''It made sense at first,'' she told him. ''I was nervous and scared, but things have changed. I can take care of myself.''

Perhaps she could, but she should not have to.

Billie used her fork to scoop up some rice. ''Can we change the subject?''

''Of course. You should try the fish. It is caught locally.''

She took a bite, then offered some to Muffin. As the dog licked her fingers, Jefri deliberately turned his mind from what had happened before. As much as he wanted justice, it was not his place.

But he wanted it to be, he realized. He wanted to

have the right to defend her with all the power at his disposal. Deep instincts, born in the darkest parts of the desert, still lived within him. He wanted to protect her as much as he wanted to claim her as his own.

He watched her move, her long bare legs a temptation no man should have to bear. He ached with his need, but whatever plans he might have had for the evening had changed. He needed time to come to terms with her past and decide how it changed things. If nothing else, he would have to move more slowly with her.

He offered her bread, then watched her take a bite. How many men had there been since that disastrous night? How many lovers?

Not many, he decided. As amazing as he found her, there was still an air of innocence about her. Between her past and her brothers, he wondered how innocent she might be.

"What?" she asked, narrowing her gaze. "Tell me exactly what you're thinking."

He shrugged. "Nothing of importance."

"Why do I know you're lying? I shouldn't have told you about what happened. You're going to get completely freaked out, aren't you?"

"Freaked out?"

"You're going to start acting as if I'm made of glass or something. This is just so typically male."

"You appear to be upset, but I have no idea of the cause."

She rose to her knees and glared at him. "You're completely weirded out and you're not going to kiss me or touch me or anything, are you? I should have guessed.''

He did his best not to smile. ''Is that what you think?''

''Absolutely. You're afraid I'll act funny or think you're attacking me. Well, I won't. That was a long time ago and I'm completely over it.''

''You think you know everything about me.''

Her mouth twisted. ''You're not that hard to read.''

''Then I will have to prove you wrong on several accounts.''

Before she could respond, he pulled her to him and kissed her.

Chapter Seven

While Billie had to admit that Jefri held her as if she were something precious, she wasn't sure any part of that was about her past. Judging from the possessive way he pulled her against him and the deepness of his kiss, she thought maybe passion had a part in it, too.

As his hands stroked her back and his mouth claimed hers, she found herself wanting to relax against him and let the moment unfold. She wanted to tell him he could touch other places than just her back, and that maybe they could do more than kiss.

Her own desires excited her as much as they made her blush. Still she didn't move away or in any other way discourage him. She wanted this man more than she'd wanted anyone in a long, long time.

Jefri tilted his head and deepened the kiss. The more he touched Billie, the more he wanted her. Her curves called out to be explored and pleasured in a thousand different ways. When his fingers tangled in her long hair, he imagined her kissing his bare chest and her long hair tickling his sides. When she wrapped her arms around his neck and her breasts pressed against him, he thought about cupping those curves, then tasting the hard, tight nipples.

Desire and need made him ache. He was hard to the point of pain. Still, he did nothing more than kiss, despite the invitation in her kisses. For one thing, he could not be sure her brother wouldn't arrive to check on his sister, and when Jefri started to make love with Billie, he did not want any interruptions. For another, he wanted to test her, to be sure she had fully recovered from her experience. If there were still scars and tender spots, he wanted to respect her boundaries.

Still, she was difficult to resist when her breath caught and she bit on his lower lip.

"You are a temptation," he said, pulling back slightly and staring into her wide eyes. "Difficult to resist."

"The same could be said about you."

He smiled. "Then we will practice self-control together."

She pouted. "Do we have to?"

"For now."

"Is that a tease or a promise?"

"Which would you like it to be?"

She took his hand and put it on her breast. The full

curve burned him down to his soul. His arousal flexed in anticipation as he brushed his thumb across her nipple.

They both sucked in a breath.

Jefri reached for her as she moved toward him. He pushed away the coffee table so they could drop to the ground in a tangle of arms and legs and violent desire. She rolled onto her back and he braced himself on one elbow so he was above her. When he slipped his hand under her T-shirt, she smiled in obvious anticipation.

A loud knock at the door interrupted them.

Jefri held in a groan. "I will guess that is your brother," he said. "I had a feeling he would check on you."

"What?" She pushed into a sitting position. "You're kidding?"

There was a second knock, followed by, "Billie, it's Doyle. I wanted to check on you."

"I'm fine. Go away."

"No. Let me in."

Jefri stood and pulled Billie to her feet.

"I'll get rid of him," she said.

He shook his head. "I will see you tomorrow."

"But…"

He took her hand in his and kissed her fingers. "Soon," he promised and walked toward the French doors where he let himself out onto the balcony.

Billie watched the prince go and could have cheerfully thrown the coffee table after him. She understood *why* he left, but she didn't have to like it.

After smoothing the front of her T-shirt to make sure everything was covered, she walked to the door and jerked it open.

"What do you want?" she demanded.

Doyle lounged in the doorway. "I'm checking on you. Dinner was great. You should have stayed."

She stalked into the center of the room, crossed her arms over her chest and glared at him. "You made that impossible. Get off of me. I mean it."

He walked toward her, stopping only a couple of feet away. "I can't help worrying."

"I appreciate that, but keep your worries to yourself. I'm a big girl. I've had sex before." Okay, only once and it had been fairly uninspiring, but her brother didn't have to know that.

Doyle winced. "Jeez, Billie. Don't tell me that."

"Why not? Isn't all this about protecting my virtue? Don't you think the prince has his choice of women? Isn't it unlikely he's going to have to force himself on anyone?" Certainly not on her. She'd been more than willing. Based on just the kissing, the event would have been fairly spectacular. Talk about lousy timing.

"I'm not worried Jefri's going to attack you. But he could break your heart. You're playing way out of your league."

"I refuse to take relationship advice from a man who has never had a serious relationship in his life."

Doyle grinned. "I run too fast to let them catch me."

"I suspect there's a deeper reason but right now

I'm too tired to figure it out. So here's the thing. I'm going to keep seeing Jefri as long as both of us are interested and you can't do anything about it. And if you continue to bug me, I will make good on my threat to leave and get a job somewhere else.''

His blue eyes, the same dark shade as her own, studied her. ''You're not kidding, are you?''

''No. It's bad enough being the only girl in this family. I won't be treated like an idiot as well.''

Her brother's shoulders slumped. ''Okay. You win. No more following you on dates. I promise.''

As Doyle had never gone back on his word before, she decided to believe him.

''Good,'' she said. ''Now I don't have to kill you.''

He grinned, then his gaze slipped past her to the coffee table. ''Leftovers, huh? Anything good?''

''Didn't you just have dinner at that restaurant?''

''Sure, but I can always eat.''

''Bank left,'' Billie said into the microphone of her headset. ''Bank, then roll. That's it, that's it. I've got you now, you thick-headed mutant.''

She heard chuckling in her headset.

''I wonder how much of your intensity has to do with making your brother suffer for what happened two nights ago.''

As always, Jefri's rich voice made her tingle. ''There's a little of that,'' she admitted as she kept her gaze on the instrument panel where she watched as the four planes converged.

''Get him,'' she said cheerfully. ''We'll do a double tone-lock. That will be very cool.''

''As you wish,'' Jefri said.

Seconds later she heard Doyle swearing as he clicked on to their communication channel.

''You did that on purpose,'' he complained.

''Doyle got beaten by a girl,'' she said in a singsong voice.

One plane instantly disappeared from her radar. Seconds later the door to the simulator jerked open and her brother glared at her.

''Don't ever say that to me again,'' he told her, doing his best to look fierce.

Billie wasn't the least bit impressed. She stuck out her tongue. ''Beat you in twenty-seven seconds. That's pretty pathetic.''

He muttered something under his breath and stalked off. Jefri took his place in the doorway.

''Remind me not to annoy you,'' he said. ''You do not seem to forgive and forget.''

''Not where my brothers are concerned. We did very well this morning.''

''I agree. I find I much prefer flying with you than against you.''

She grinned. ''A wise man.''

''I thought we might try dinner again tonight. Are you available?''

She was more than available, she was practically at the point of begging. ''I could make the time.''

''Good. I have a plan to avoid the press.''

"Which is?"

"We are going to another country."

That evening they flew over the desert in a private luxury jet, although neither of them were at the controls. Billie fingered her curls, hoping her hair was big enough for the significance of the event and took the glass of champagne Jefri offered.

"So this is why we're not flying ourselves," she said.

"Absolutely."

She took a sip and tried not to read too much into Jefri's smoldering looks, while ignoring the way her thighs kept going up in flames.

It was all too much, she thought as she took in the rich leather interior of the jet. Too much luxury, too much man and way too much class. He looked amazing in his tailored dark suit. After the last debacle, Billie had given up on original and had slipped into a simple, black cocktail dress. She felt she looked good, but what did she know about a prince's expectations?

"So, where are we going?" she asked more to distract herself than because she cared about the destination.

"El Bahar."

"Oh. They're not that far away."

"Agreed, but no one should bother us there."

"I've never been, but I've heard it's very beautiful. Too bad it's night, we're missing the desert."

"You can fly over it any time you would like."

''Not all of it,'' she said with a smile. ''There is some very restricted airspace out there.''

Oddly enough in the middle of nowhere. She'd noticed it the first time she'd planned her flight in to Bahania.

''What on earth are you keeping hidden in the middle of the desert?''

She expected a teasing response. Instead Jefri studied her intently. ''It is a secret.''

''What kind? Military?''

He shook his head. ''We think of it as a treasure.''

She tried to imagine what it could be. What kind of treasure could exist such that planes couldn't fly overhead?

As she sipped more champagne, she thought about her research on the area and recalled mention of a fabled city—The City of Thieves.

No. That wasn't possible. A secret city?

''Is it bigger than a bread box?'' she asked.

He smiled. ''Much.''

''If I drove there instead of trying to fly there, could I see it?''

''What would you like to see?''

''I'm not sure.''

''When you decide, we'll talk about it.''

''You're not exactly what I expected,'' she told him. ''I thought a prince would be different.''

''In what way?''

''I'm not sure.''

''I am simply a man, like many others.''

"Actually, you're not, but that's okay."

He leaned close and brushed his mouth against hers. "I am glad."

Billie wasn't surprised to find a limo waiting for them at the airport. They'd come into a private field next to the main international airport. Jefri had warned her to bring her passport, but their trip through customs was a simple walk past uniformed officials who bowed and offered greetings of welcome.

She and her royal date were whisked into the center of the brightly lit city where they stopped in front of a small restaurant.

"No cameras in sight," she said as she stepped out onto the sidewalk. "I like this much better."

"Many women enjoy being the center of attention," he said.

"Then I say they should go for it. I'm not into the whole 'center of a crowd' thing. I get nervous."

They walked inside and were quickly shown to a private table tucked into an alcove. Billie did a quick visual search of nearby tables before she took her seat.

"No paparazzi and no brother," she said. "This is my idea of a good time."

"I am glad you approve."

Jefri ordered wine, they discussed the menu, but all the while, she couldn't stop thinking about how amazing this was. She was out to dinner with a man who had flown her to another country for the meal because he was a prince and they couldn't go out to eat where he lived. Jefri was royal, as in his daddy owned a palace and everything.

"What is wrong?" he asked when the waiter had left with their order. "You have gone pale."

"I think I just completely grasped who you are."

"In what way?"

She waved her fingers. "Let's start with something easier. Who *I* am. My father owns a successful company. We've always done well, but we're not exactly rolling in money. I grew up surrounded by planes and burly mechanics. I did my entire high school education by correspondence. I know more about going Mach 4 than ballroom dancing and in stressful social situations, I usually put my foot in my mouth."

He leaned toward her and captured her hand. "What is your point?"

She laughed. "That I can't figure out what you're doing with me. I saw the magazine articles and the type of women you usually date. They're gorgeous. Movie stars and divas and daughters of really, really rich men."

"I see. And you do not consider yourself like them?"

"I can hold my own." Sort of. "It's just weird."

"Two nights ago you accused me of being 'weirded out' about your past. You have a fondness for the word."

She sighed. "See. I can't even speak correctly."

He kissed her fingers, which made her heart do the happy dance.

"You do extremely well. I am delighted to be with you and honored by your presence."

"Jeez, do you know how to get the girls or what?"

"You doubt my sincerity."

"Not at all. I'm just trying to keep up."

"This is not a competition, and my world is not all you think it to be. I was sent away to a British boarding school when I was nine years old. At seventeen, I went to America, to college. My brother, Reyhan, had made the mistake of letting people know who he was when he first entered college, so he was followed and judged and kept in the press for the entire four years." He kissed her fingers again. "I learned from his mistake and decided to keep my identity a secret."

She could imagine the feeding frenzy as the coeds found out there was a single royal prince on campus. "Did it work?"

He nodded. "I managed to get through with only a few close friends finding out. I met women who were interested in me for myself." He smiled. "It was a most humbling experience."

"I doubt that." He was the sort of man women would want regardless of his royal status.

"When I reached twenty-one, women descended on Bahania. They wanted the opportunity to marry a prince. I am not sure what I wanted, but they were not it. Still, some played the game very well and I was fooled more than once."

"That's understandable." The combination of willing women and the natural desire to believe it was all about him could have made things very complicated.

"I married one of them," he said.

The statement was so unexpected that had she been drinking she would have spit.

"You what?"

He looked at her as he rubbed her fingers. "From what I could see, she was perfect. Beautiful, well mannered. There was some trace of European royalty in her heritage, her father controlled multinational banks. It was a match that delighted everyone involved."

Married? As in… She carefully withdrew her hand. "You're not married now, are you?"

He took her hand in his and smiled. "No. I am not married now."

"But you were?"

"Yes. We were married. The wedding was a state occasion and it only took me six months to realize my wife had a heart of stone."

Billie had done some reading about Jefri, but none of the articles had mentioned a wife. "You're divorced?"

He nodded. "She was not someone I wanted to be the mother of my children."

That sounded a little imperious but she understood his point. "Was it really hard to get over her?" she asked, liking how he kept circling her palm with his thumb. "I mean with your heart broken and all."

"My heart was not broken."

"I don't understand. You can't just turn off love."

"I did not love her."

The waiter arrived with their bottle of red wine, which gave Billie some time to work on getting over being stunned. Jefri didn't love the woman he married?

"How is that possible?" she asked when they were alone again. "She was your wife."

"Yes, and she could have been the mother of my children. There can be respect and mutual understanding, but love is not required."

"Hello? I've seen your brothers. They're wildly in love with their wives." So much so that she'd felt a twinge of envy.

"There is passion between them," he admitted. "But love? I doubt it."

"I… You…" She grabbed her wineglass. "That's just crazy. How can you marry someone you don't love?"

"A royal match has certain requirements from both parties."

"What about being swept away? What about wanting to be with someone so much you can't think of anything else?"

His eyes darkened. "That I completely agree with. Despite these trappings of civility, I am at heart, a man of the desert. My blood runs hot."

She nearly dropped her glass. They'd gone from talking to something very different in the space of a heartbeat.

"You know what I want," he said, his voice low. "Tell me what you desire. If it is for me to leave you alone, you only have to speak the words."

And if it isn't? But she already knew the answer to that. No one had ever asked her a question like that. No one had put it all on the line. She felt Jefri's barely concealed passion and it excited her. That he wanted her enough to plainly state it made her quiver.

As for her... She knew her heart's desire. The sensible side of her brain warned her that there was no happy ending in this. That if she allowed herself to care, she would only get her heart broken. She knew who and what he was as well as she knew she would never fit in his world. Worse, he was a man who had married because it was the right thing to do, and not for love. She wanted a husband who was completely devoted to her and their family.

So this wasn't going to lead to a happily ever after. Was she still willing to take what he offered?

She stared into his eyes. "All my life I've been fearless in the skies. There is no plane I won't fly, no barrier I'm not willing to break through."

But in her personal life, she'd allowed herself to be ruled by her brothers' pronouncements and maybe a little by her own fear.

"I don't want you to leave me alone," she said, her voice barely a whisper.

"Are you sure? We can call for the plane or stay the night."

She glanced around at the elegant restaurant. "Right here?"

He smiled. "I have a villa on the edge of the sea. It's beautiful and private."

She knew what she wanted. One night with him would be a memory she would always treasure.

"A villa, huh? Do you want to go now, or do you want to wait until after dinner?"

Jefri stared at her for several seconds, then raised his hand to the waiter. "We would like the check, please."

Chapter Eight

If she'd had time to picture a villa owned by a sheik, she wouldn't have been able to imagine a place as beautiful as the one on the edge of the sea. Their car dropped them off in front and Jefri used a key to let them in.

From the foyer, she could see through to the dark lapping ocean. The marble floor was the color of the inside of an oyster shell, the walls, a pale peach. Instead of overhead lights, there were candles everywhere. Candles and rose petals and the scent of promise.

"You planned this," she said, not sure if she should be upset or not.

"I hoped. There is a difference."

He came up behind her and placed his hands on

her shoulders. At the same time he moved her hair aside, then leaned down and lightly kissed her neck. Instantly her skin puckered and her blood heated. She felt the desire course through her. Muscles tensed and between her legs, a faint throbbing began.

She decided she needed to keep her wits about her as long as possible. Even if that meant only for the next fifteen seconds.

"So, ah, do you bring women here often?" she asked.

He chuckled as he kissed his way to her spine. "You are my first, but not *the* first. This villa belongs to the king of El Bahar. It was built nearly five centuries ago as a home for the king's mistress."

He whispered the words in her ear, then lightly bit her earlobe.

"Because a harem isn't enough?" she asked, barely able to speak.

"This offers what the harem does not. Privacy."

Ah, yes. Something that seemed like a very good idea.

"So you called him early today and said 'Hey, Your Highness, I have this girl I'd like to impress. Mind if I use the love shack?' Or words to that effect?"

Jefri turned her in his arms so they stared at each other. "Why do you mock me?"

"Because I'm nervous. Is that against the law?"

He smiled. "Not at all, but I may have to punish you for your impertinence."

"Really? What does that involve?"

"Let me show you."

He bent down and kissed her. In the nanosecond before their lips touched, she tensed in anticipation. Then, when he brushed his mouth against hers, she couldn't help melting against him, letting her body sag against his as he claimed her.

She parted for him, wanting him to deepen the kiss. She wrapped her arms around his neck and savored his eagerness as he pulled her hard against him.

He was strong, she thought, her mind blurring with need. Hard to her yielding. Her breasts nestled against the planes of his chest. Her stomach pillowed the hard proof of his desire. When she clamped her lips around his tongue, he pulsed against her, delighting her with the promise of feminine power.

"Are you all right?" he asked as he broke the kiss and pressed his mouth to her jaw. "Does any of this make you nervous?"

She shifted her hands to his face and cupped his cheeks. He straightened and looked at her.

"I'm not afraid," she told him as she stared into his passion-filled eyes. "Jefri, I'm not a virgin." Funny how this was the second time in as many days that she'd made the announcement. Until now, it hadn't been an issue in years.

"After I'd been attacked, I really withdrew from men and dating," she continued. "Then I realized I couldn't keep doing that, so I deliberately set out to get a boyfriend. We were in Australia for a few months and I met someone there. He was sweet and very gentle. Anyway, we became lovers."

She remembered being awkward and scared and all the things Jefri feared she would be with him. She had a feeling that Andrew had been as inexperienced as she had been. They'd fumbled through making love several times before she'd left the country.

"My point is, I've done this before."

His dark gaze gave nothing away. "And since that first lover? Have there been many?"

"Um, well, not exactly. But that's not because I was afraid."

"Lack of opportunity or lack of interest?" he asked.

"A little of both."

"I see."

He spoke the words with a confidence that came from…actually she wasn't sure what, but it made her shiver in anticipation.

"Thank you for letting me know I do not have to worry about your past," he said as he took her hand and led her down a short hallway. "Still, it is my nature to take things slowly at first. I hope you will indulge me."

"Of course." After all, what did she know about the whole process? Well, the basics, of course, but she had a feeling that Jefri's lovemaking would be nothing like Andrew's.

They walked into a large bedroom. Rose petals littered the marble floor. In the corner stood a massive tub filled with rose-scented water. Steam rose toward the painted ceiling. A bed filled the center of the room. Cream-colored linens invited her to touch. A netted canopy offered the illusion of privacy. Here as in the main room of the house, candles provided flickering light.

"For your hair," Jefri said, handing her several clips.

She saw he'd taken them from a carved dresser by the door.

She twisted her long curls into a coil and pinned it up on her head. When she'd finished, he shrugged out of his jacket and left it on a chair.

"We're getting in that, aren't we?" she asked, pointing at the tub.

"If you do not mind."

"Before or, after, you know."

He smiled. "Before. You may step behind that screen and undress," he said and pointed.

She followed his gaze and saw a painted screen concealing a corner. Huh. She'd assumed he was going to be taking her clothes off. She wasn't sure if she was relieved or disappointed to be doing it herself.

Still she walked behind the screen where she found a chair and a silk robe waiting. She stepped out of her shoes, then unfastened her dress and carefully hung it up. Her bra and panties followed. When she was naked, she slipped on the robe.

The silk was cool and soft against her heated skin, but even the delicate fabric seemed to tease her tight nipples. The sensation was both pleasurable and frustrating.

When she walked out from behind the screen, she

saw Jefri also in a robe, although his was black and hers pale pink. He motioned to the tub.

She moved closer, then hesitated, not sure about getting into the deep, hot water in front of him. But he came up behind her and reached around her to unfasten her robe, not giving her a whole lot of choice.

Clenching her teeth against potential embarrassment, she shrugged out of the garment and stepped into the steaming tub. First one foot, then the other.

"You are incredible," he said, his voice nearly a growl.

Billie looked up only to stare at a reflection of herself. She'd been too focused on the water to notice the mirror behind the tub. She glanced over and met his passionate gaze in the glass. Then he dropped the robe and moved close.

"I must touch you," he breathed. "For a moment. Please."

She was unable to move, barely able to breathe. He put his hands on her waist, then moved one up and one down. The fingers on one hand reached her breast at the same movement fingers on the other slipped between her thighs. She was already wet, swollen and ready. The combination of touches with the visual before her made her want to swoon.

"Exquisite," he murmured before he kissed her neck. "How soft you are. Your skin." He brushed his thumb against her tight left nipple. "Your secrets." He slid fingers in deeper.

One brushed against that single point of pleasure

and she jumped. He bit her shoulder, then smiled at her in the mirror.

"I want to please you," he told her. "All of you."

Who was she to argue? she thought as he stepped back and she sank into the hot water.

She figured he would join her, but he didn't. Instead he moved behind her so when she stretched out, her head rested against his chest.

A tray sat next to the tub. He picked up the first bottle and opened it.

"What do you think?" he asked, letting her smell the orange-spicy scent.

"It's nice."

"I want more of a reaction than that." He continued to open bottles for her until a musky-floral scent got her attention.

"That one," she said.

"Good."

He poured some lotion onto his hands and rubbed his palms together. She'd expected soap but the liquid didn't lather. Instead it thickened and glistened like some kind of oil.

This entire experience was so out of her regular world, she didn't know what to think. But if this was basic prince seduction, then someone had to sign her up for at least a monthly session.

Jefri slipped his hands under the water and moved toward her breasts. When his palms cupped her curves, she realized the lotion was an oil. A slick, warm concoction that didn't dissolve in water and made her nerve endings even more sensitive than usual.

He circled around her breasts as if discovering every inch of them. Around and around, without touching her tight nipples. She squirmed and ached and shifted in the water, but still he touched only the pale flesh, leaving the tips mournfully alone.

Heat poured through her. Need built. He kissed her neck so lightly when she wanted to beg him to do more. Touch more, bite more, something. Anything!

At last he stroked her nipples and she nearly cried out in relief. He rolled them between his thumb and forefinger, sending ribbons of pleasure directly down her chest, through her stomach and between her legs. She ached there. She ached everywhere. She wanted with a desperation that nearly frightened her.

Arousal poured through her body, making her writhe. At last she couldn't stay silent.

"More," she pleaded.

"Yes. Move forward."

Then his hands were gone. She grasped the sides of the tub and slid toward the other end. At the same time she turned to look in the mirror as Jefri stood and dropped his robe.

He stood there naked and aroused. His need jutted forward proudly, making her want to part her legs and beg him to take her. Instead she waited while he stepped in behind her and sank into the tub.

The two of them fit easily. He pulled her against him so her back settled against his chest. His erection pressed against her back, which wasn't the least bit satisfying, but she found she didn't mind so much when he once again slipped a hand between her legs.

She closed her eyes as he began to touch her. He found that one perfect place at once and gently rubbed it. Her breath caught, then she couldn't breathe at all. Faster, she thought. No, slower. No, just like that.

She arched into his touch, wanting all of it. Tension filled her body. She clutched the side of the tub and let herself experience the steady build toward—

He put a hand on her breasts. One second he hadn't been touching her there and the next he was matching his movements and she lost control.

Her orgasm crashed into her with no warning. Suddenly her body convulsed into exquisite pleasure. The waves of her pleasure shuddered through her over and over until at last they slowed.

She returned to consciousness only to find the water in the tub still shifting back and forth. His hand still stroked her between her legs and she was slightly embarrassed to feel herself getting aroused again.

"You should probably, you know, stop," she said although she didn't push him away.

"Why?" he asked. "I like touching you."

"And you're really good at it."

"Turn around," he said.

She did as he requested, only to find herself straddling him. His dark gaze dropped to where her breasts floated in the water.

"You are a fantasy come to life," he said.

"As are you."

He pulled her close and they kissed. His arousal

rubbed between her legs, exciting her. She wanted to shift just enough for him to slip inside, but before she could, he pushed her back.

"This was only the appetizer," he said as he stood.

He stood dripping and naked while he collected a towel for her and gently wrapped it around her. Only then did he claim one for himself. He dried every inch of her before escorting her to the bed where he had her stretch out on her back. From a carved nightstand he produced a condom, but he didn't slip it on. Instead he knelt between her ankles and gently kissed her instep.

From there he made his way to her shin, then her knee. He repeated the procedure on her other leg, but this time moving higher and higher still.

She didn't know what to think, what to say, so she decided only to feel. No one had ever done this to her before. She'd never really understood the combination of vulnerability and amazing pleasure when a man's mouth pressed an open kiss on the very heart of her.

Her breath caught as her body went up in flames. It was too much. It would never be enough. She ached, she burned, she wanted.

Words spilled out of her, but she had no idea what she said. He licked her everywhere, then settled on that one amazing place. At the same time, he slipped a finger inside of her and caressed her from underneath. The combination nearly made her faint.

This time she was determined to hold back as long as possible, or two minutes, whichever came first.

But there was no denying the sensations flooding

her body. Holding back her release was like trying to stop a tornado—foolish and potentially dangerous. She gave herself up to his mouth, his hands and when the first shudder of her orgasm claimed her, she gave in to the need to scream.

It was nearly an out-of-body experience, she thought, barely conscious as every cell in her body gave itself up to the magic of what he did to her. Even when the pleasure eased a little, he continued to move his finger in and out of her, making her come again and again, if not as intensely.

He drew away. She wanted to protest, only she couldn't speak or move. She was boneless, barely conscious. Then she felt something wonderfully hot and thick probing between her legs. She forced herself to open her eyes and watch as he entered her.

She climaxed again on the first full stroke of penetration. Echoing shudders claimed her as he filled her fully, as he breathed her name and moved in and out. Time ceased to have meaning. She clung to him, wanting him to find pleasure in her and relaxing with contentment as he stiffened and was still.

"Obviously I need to get out more," Billie said a few minutes later when they'd cleaned up and retreated under the covers. "I'm not sure that many orgasms in a single event is even legal."

"You are a powerful and sensual woman," Jefri told her as he brushed a kiss across her mouth. "There is much more for you to discover."

She appreciated him not making her feel freaky

about what had just happened. Frankly, she could probably live another four hundred years and never feel this good.

"You're pretty amazing yourself," she said. "I think a lot of what happened was because of you."

"I can prove you are wrong," he said. "You are delightfully responsive. I simply unlocked what is already there." He smiled. "Shall I show you?"

By ten the next morning Billie knew that she would probably walk funny for the next six weeks, but it had been worth it. Spending the night with Jefri had been beyond description. What made it even better was the slightly glazed look in his eyes whenever he turned in her direction.

"You have destroyed me for other women," he said as he held her close on the flight back to Bahania.

There was a sentiment she could get behind, she thought happily. "Me, too. Although not with women."

"Of course not."

She sighed with contentment and wondered if her smile was as happily foolish as it felt.

"Doyle's going to kill me," she said. "After he has his heart attack."

"Because you did not go home last night?"

"I'm not sure he'll care about that, but he'll be seriously unamused that I missed our morning classes."

"Shall I explain that it was with my express permission?" Jefri asked.

Billie giggled. "I'm not so sure that's a really good idea. After all, he's my brother and when he figures out what we've been doing, he may feel obligated to beat you up."

"He will not be successful."

"I suspect you're right. But it could create an international incident and we don't want that."

Jefri kissed the top of her head. "I have some meetings this afternoon, but I would like to see you tonight."

"Me, too."

"Dinner in your room?"

"Uh-huh." Dinner and then…

The plane landed at the private airport where another limo waited to take them back to the palace. Billie tried to get her brother on the cell phone, but he didn't answer.

"Strange," she said as she checked her battery. "I can't figure out why he's not picking up. He's not scheduled to fly. Maybe he's somewhere without cell coverage." Although she couldn't imagine where that would be.

"Once we are back at the palace, we will find him," Jefri told her.

She nodded and slipped into his embrace. He pressed his mouth to hers, deepening the kiss until she wanted to ask the driver to pull over and give them a minute.

Tonight, she promised herself. They would make love tonight.

Their limo pulled up behind another one.

"A visiting dignitary?" she asked as he reached for the door handle.

"I had not heard of one on the schedule." He stepped out, then turned to assist her.

As Billie walked toward the entrance to the palace, she heard loud voices. Was that—

"Doyle?"

She hurried toward the sound and came to a dead stop when she saw her brother apparently arguing with the king.

"This can't be good," she murmured. Had her brother seriously freaked out when she hadn't come home? "Doyle, what's going on?"

He spun toward her. "There you are. Where the hell have you been?"

Billie was aware of the crowd of people standing around, including a young woman of about seventeen or eighteen.

"I'm fine. Thanks for asking. How are you?"

Her brother glared at her. "I didn't ask you how you are."

"I know but things would be a whole lot better if you did."

Just then Jefri came up and put his arm around her. "What seems to be the problem?"

Doyle's gaze narrowed. "Why don't you ask your father there? Or her?" He pointed accusingly at the young woman.

"Who's she?" Billie asked.

Doyle's expression darkened as his eyes narrowed. "Prince Jefri's fiancée."

Chapter Nine

Jefri stared at the small group of people all looking at him, but he only cared about the accusation in Billie's gaze.

His fiancée?

"It is not true," he said quickly. "I have never seen this young woman before."

But even as he spoke the words, an awful truth formed. What had his father done?

"On the contrary," Doyle said, sounding furious. "Everyone seems very sure about this."

Jefri wanted to take Billie away and explain. More than that he wanted to turn back time so he could prevent this moment or at least prepare for it. Neither seemed possible.

"Hello, my dear," the king said to Billie as he took

her hand in greeting. "Welcome back. I hope you enjoyed your time in El Bahar."

"What?" Billie looked stunned. "Ah, yes. Thank you. It was great." Her expression said the emphasis was on the past tense. Things were great no longer. She looked at him, then at the young woman.

"I have to go," she said and bolted from the room.

Jefri took a step to follow her, but Doyle stepped in the way.

"Don't even think about it," Billie's brother said with a growl.

Jefri was not the least bit concerned about Doyle. He had to get to Billie and explain. There was only one problem—he wasn't sure what had occurred.

"Father?"

The king smiled. "My son, this is Tahira." The king motioned to the young girl who hovered at the edge of the foyer.

Jefri studied her. She was young, perhaps sixteen or seventeen, and very petite. She barely came to the center of his chest and her body appeared small and childlike. Dark hair had been pulled back into a simple braid. She wore no makeup, no jewelry and only a plain dark dress that covered her to well below the knees.

Jefri nodded at the girl, a pointless gesture as she did not look up from her careful study of the floor, then turned his attention to his father. "There has been a mistake."

"I think not, but regardless, this is not the place to have that discussion."

His father was right in that.

Jefri walked over to Doyle. "I never asked for her," he said. "I do not know why she is here."

Billie's brother drew his blond eyebrows together. "Is she or is she not your fiancée?"

There were technicalities involved in that question, Jefri realized. Without speaking to his father, he didn't know the truth. "I am not sure."

Doyle swore, then moved close. "Don't think this is finished, Your Highness. I don't give a damn about who or what you are. You've hurt my sister and you're going to pay for that."

Doyle stalked off in the direction Billie had fled.

"A most interesting young man," the king said and smiled at the girl. "Come, Tahira. We will adjourn to one of the small sitting rooms.

Jefri followed his father down the main corridor, then along a smaller hallway. When they entered the aforementioned room, he carefully closed the door before turning on his father.

"What have you done?" he demanded.

"As you requested. I have found you a bride."

Tahira stood by the window, her narrow shoulders hunched. Aware that she listened to every word, he lowered his voice.

"We discussed this matter recently," Jefri said. "I requested you unmake whatever the arrangements might be."

"I recall. However, things had progressed too far. When Tahira turned eighteen, she was required to leave the school."

Eighteen? Jefri glanced at the young woman. Was it possible she was that old?

The king smiled in her direction. "Come, child. It is time to properly meet your husband-to-be."

Tahira obediently walked to the king. When she raised her head, Jefri caught side of large brown eyes brilliant with terror. She swallowed and lowered her chin.

"Prince Jefri. I have no words to express my honor and joy at finally meeting you."

If this was joy, he would hate to see her upset. "Tahira…" He hesitated. None of this was the girl's fault. "The honor is mine," he said, trying not to sound grim.

"She has been in the convent school on Lucia-Serrat," the king said. "Her father was my finance minister until he was killed in a car accident when she was only seven. He was a dear friend and his wish was for me to provide for his only child."

Jefri knew enough to read between the lines. Tahira had no one. There might or might not be any money from her family, but that did not matter. The king had sent her to the convent school where she would be well educated in the social graces, cooking and child-rearing, if not in the ways of the world. He doubted she had ever seen a man his age before.

Whether his father had originally planned for her to marry one of his sons or he had thought to offer Tahira in marriage to some highly placed official, obviously, she had not been prepared to make her way in the world on her own.

"She speaks several languages," the king continued. "The sisters also said you were gifted in sketching and painting. Is that not so, child?"

Tahira barely nodded. "The sisters were kind to me and offered many compliments, Your Highness. I would not dare to say I have talent."

"Of course not," Jefri murmured, wondering if there was a way out of this hell.

"She meets all your requirements," the king said. "She is very pretty."

Hard to know, what with her still staring at the floor, Jefri thought. Although her appearance was the least of it.

He had to get to Billie and explain. He had to make this right with her.

"You have arranged rooms?" he asked his father.

"Of course. Something with a view of the gardens. I thought Tahira would find that familiar. You had beautiful gardens at the school, did you not?"

Tahira nodded.

Jefri swore silently. "I must excuse myself," he told his father, then glanced at the girl. "Welcome to Bahania," he said stiffly and hurried out of the room.

He made his way to the third floor and Billie's suite. As he turned the corner, he saw Doyle lounging by the door. The large man stepped into the corridor and smiled coldly.

"I figured you'd come sniffing around here," Doyle said angrily. "She's not here and I'm not telling you where she is. What I will tell you is you're the lowest form of life there is. This may cost my family the contract and me my freedom, but I plan to beat the crap out of you. Prince or not, you don't have the right to act like this.''

Gone? Where could she be? Jefri thought of the possibilities and decided Billie would retreat to the airport and the Van Horn complex there.

''Are you listening to me?'' Doyle demanded.

''No,'' Jefri told him. ''But I understand your fury. I have two sisters and I would do the same for them. The problem is you are not in a position to beat the crap out of me.''

Doyle narrowed his gaze. ''You think I care that it's against the law?''

Jefri did not have time for this but he knew Doyle would not let him walk away until this was resolved.

Jefri moved close to the other man. They were about the same height and size. ''Do not let the tailored suits fool you, Doyle. I have been trained by masters. You will not get off the first punch.''

Doyle's hands curled into fists.

Jefri shook his head. ''You must believe me. I would never hurt her.''

''Too late for that. Where the hell do you get the right to take her away for the night? She's not your plaything.''

''I agree. She is an amazing woman who constantly surprises me. Now I must find her and explain.''

''There's no way she'll forgive you.''

''That information will not stop me from trying.''

Doyle flexed his fingers. ''If she's still mad when you're done, then you and I are having it out. Just so we're clear. And for what it's worth, you'd better have a hell of a good story.''

Jefri nodded, then left. He raced down to the garages where he collected his Jaguar and headed for the airport. He didn't have a story at all. He only had the truth. But would it be enough?

Billie found that reaching a personal best on a video game where she saved the world from outer space-based villains didn't make her feel any better. She was a little surprised she'd done so well, what with the tears blurring her vision. There wasn't a single part of her that didn't hurt. Even her eyelashes ached. Her body felt pummeled and her heart… She didn't want to think about the damage done to that organ.

Funny how she'd tried to prepare herself for the reality of her situation with Jefri. She'd thought she'd known who and what he was. A prince. Not the kind of guy a woman like her had a chance with. She'd accepted theirs would be an affair and she'd been happy with that. But finding out he'd been engaged the entire time made her feel slimy and gross. As if she were the other woman. Which she very well was.

How could he have done that? She would never have guessed he was that kind of man. He'd struck her as honorable, which just went to show she was an idiot.

It hurt, she thought, as fresh tears spilled down her cheeks. This hurt more than anything, even that night when those guys had gone for her. They'd tried to damage her body, but Jefri had messed with her head and her heart.

She brushed her hand against her face and concentrated on the screen. More spaceships flew into view. She began to systematically fire at them, racking up points like crazy. All the explosions and sound effects from the machine provided a comforting blanket of white noise, but they didn't prevent her from hearing steady footsteps on the concrete floor.

Every muscle in her body tensed. She knew who approached even before he spoke. The need to run overwhelmed her, but she had a feeling he wasn't willing to let her grieve in peace. Instead he would want to have his say and make it right. How like a man. Just once, she would like to see one of them take responsibility instead of weaseling out of everything.

"I know what you are thinking," Jefri said when he came to a stop behind her.

"Somehow I doubt that."

She hated that she didn't have to turn to know it was him. Her heart sensed his presence.

"You are thinking that I am a lying, cheating bastard who used you to get what he wanted. You are thinking you were tricked."

She released her hands from the controls and let the aliens claim her last ship. With her eyes closed, she did her best to keep breathing.

"Pretty close," she admitted.

"Billie, you have to believe me. I did not plan for any of this to happen. Not you and what we did last night and certainly not that scene today. I would never hurt you.''

She drew in a deep breath and wiped her face before turning to face him. Her stomach flinched when she realized he was still gorgeous. Turning into scum hadn't affected his looks.

"Imagine what you could do if you tried," she said, doing her best to hold the tears at bay and keep her voice steady. "With a little effort, you could do a serious number on my heart."

He reached out to touch her, but she stepped back. "Don't do that," she said.

"You are right. I apologize."

She nodded stiffly. "So what exactly is the purpose of this visit?"

"To explain."

"Are you or are you not engaged?"

"The situation is more complex than that."

"Funny, because from where I stand, it seems fairly simple. Just answer the question."

He shoved his hands into his front pockets. "I am Prince Jefri of Bahania."

"I already know that, but thanks for sharing."

His steady gaze locked on her face. "My father expects me to produce heirs. After my disastrous first marriage, I decided that I was not the best judge of who I should claim as my wife, so I agreed to let my father arrange a match."

Billie heard the words but had a heck of a time believing them. "You're willing to marry someone you've never met?"

He shrugged. "At the time it seemed a simple solution to a problem I did not want to deal with."

"We're talking about your entire life. This is the woman you'll grow old with. She'll be the mother of your children."

"Exactly." His dark eyes narrowed. "I wanted the right woman to give me strong sons and daughters. My father would be able to learn about her family, her education. What she would be like as a mother."

Billie thought about pointing out Jefri could do the same if he would simply invest a little time.

"Let me see if I get this straight. The king wanted you to marry and you told him that if it was so important, he could take care of finding you the bride himself."

"Yes."

"That's insane. What if you hate her?"

"My father would ensure compatibility. The point is a few weeks ago my father mentioned he'd found me a bride. I told him I did not want any arrangements made. I assumed the matter was closed. But I was wrong."

Billie stared at him. "If you're lying…"

"I give you my word. I did not know about Tahira yesterday."

She supposed that was something. At least he wasn't a complete bastard. "And now?"

He hesitated long enough to make her furious.

"What?" she demanded. "Are you engaged or not?"

"As I said, the situation is complicated."

"By what?"

"Tahira herself. She was raised in a particular way."

"What? By wolves?"

"Nuns."

Billie took a step back. "Are you telling me this girl is fresh from the convent?"

He nodded.

"Great. Let me guess the rest. She has no family, nowhere to go and golly, she's been trained to be the perfect princess."

He sighed. "Why do I know your understanding is not a good thing?"

"Because you're not always an idiot. So what exactly makes her the perfect princess?" Billie couldn't remember anything about the girl. Just that she'd been painfully young.

"She is all I requested."

Not sure she wanted to hear this, she still insisted, "Give me specifics."

"I requested a wife who was reasonably attractive with a docile temperament and a fondness for children."

She blinked. "What? You asked for that? This is a marriage, not eBay. You can't just place an order and then wait for the future princess to be delivered."

"Why not?"

Billie wished she was big enough to slap him and have it hurt. Worse, she hated the sudden need to smash in his perfect face, but she couldn't seem to shake it, either. She thought briefly about her high-heeled sandal, but didn't think she was strong enough to actually pierce stupid, male flesh with the heel.

"I do not expect to love her," Jefri said as if that explained everything. "Ours would be a marriage of convenience."

"Tell me about it. A marriage in the tradition of all great misogynistic monarchies. I'm sure you'll enjoy sleeping with your reasonably attractive, docile wife and that together you'll produce reasonably attractive, docile children."

"You do not understand."

"I understand perfectly. That's not a marriage and it's sure as hell no way to live a life. If that's what you want, you're not the man I thought."

She clung to that revelation and hoped it would be enough to help her get over him. Gathering her tattered dignity, she headed for the exit.

Unfortunately Jefri wasn't going to allow her a clean getaway. Instead he followed, keeping up with her easily.

"You are angry," he said.

"Thanks for the news flash."

"In time you will understand."

She doubted that. Her fantasy was that in time he wouldn't matter to her. Not that he mattered now. Okay, they'd had some laughs and a really fabulous night, but that didn't mean anything. She hadn't fallen for him.

He reached for her arm. She spun toward him.

"Don't touch me," she said, her voice low and angry. "You no longer have the right."

"Billie, you have to be reasonable."

"I don't think so. I don't think I have to be anything I don't want to be, and certainly not because you said so."

"Please. You mean the world to me."

"Ha! Even if I believed you, I wouldn't care. If you need a woman, I suggest you go check out Miss Docile and Reasonably Attractive. I'm sure she'll welcome you with open arms."

Chapter Ten

Billie hid out at the airport for another hour, but knew she couldn't stay there forever. Not unless she planned on moving back. The option gave her pause—was she willing to give up the perfect bathroom because of a broken heart? She quickly decided that living tubless would only add to her pain, so better to be at the palace and suffering than in a tent and hating life.

Once back at the palace, she found herself unable to stay in her room, so she collected Muffin and hurried toward the garden. Maybe being outside in something so beautiful would ease her spirits.

"I didn't expect to recover in fifteen seconds," she told her dog as she set her down on the path. "But I would appreciate being able to breathe without shooting pains in my chest."

Muffin gave her a quick sympathetic look before hurrying off to check out the nearby plants and shrubs. Billie sank onto a stone bench and contemplated her options.

She could leave. Contract or no contract, she could simply walk away from the job.

As soon as the thought formed, she dismissed it. She didn't run away and she didn't quit. Which left her in the unique position of having to regularly see the man who had hurt her.

Could she do it? ''Dumb question,'' she murmured. ''Of course I can do it. The trick will be doing it well.''

She probed at the open wounds to gauge their depth. How long until she recovered? How long until she was able to look back at all this and know it had been an important lesson for her to learn? If nothing else, the sex had been fabulous. She'd figured out she had the kind of body that responded really well to the right sort of touch. Maybe she should stop thinking about Jefri and start figuring out who she could find to replace him. Would taking another lover make her feel better?

She wasn't sure of the answer to the question, but the thought of another man doing what he had done made her stomach roll. Okay, so she would need a little time and distance before searching out another lover. That was fine. She had time.

Muffin trotted past on her way to another tree where a long sniffing session was in order. Billie watched her, then stiffened when she heard footsteps on the path. Her heart fluttered, then slowed when she realized they didn't belong to Jefri.

How horrible that her world had been reduced to him or not him. Funny how she hadn't known she was involved and now she had to work on getting over him.

The king rounded the corner in the path and moved toward her. Billie knew bolting wasn't an option so she braced herself for the interruption and rose to her feet.

"Please," he said as he waved her back onto her seat. "Do you mind a little company?"

"Of course not, Your Highness."

He sat next to her and took her hand. "I will admit that spending time with such a beautiful young woman brightens my day."

She did her best to smile. "While I appreciate the compliment, you're in a position of great power. Doesn't that mean you can get all the young women you want?"

He raised his eyebrows. "You are right. I had forgotten. I will see to acquiring as many as possible this very afternoon."

Her smile turned genuine. "That would make for an interesting to-do list."

"I agree. My staff would not know what had happened to me." He patted her hand, then released it. "Tell me about the training. It goes well?"

"Yes. You have excellent pilots in the program." None better than Jefri, but she wasn't going to talk about him if she could help it. "We're taking their individual strengths and honing them, while shoring up weaknesses. At the same time, we're working on making them a team. Your deserts will be well protected from the skies.''

"That is good to hear.'' The king sighed. ''Times changed. A hundred years ago could anyone have imagined having to patrol the deserts in such a fashion?''

''Probably not. But change isn't always bad.''

''I agree. We must keep up with the times, as they say. Move forward. Invest in our future.''

''Is that what Tahira is?'' she asked before she could stop herself. ''An investment in the future?''

She kept her gaze on Muffin rather than the king, but she felt the monarch study her.

''I am an old man,'' he said. ''Is it so wrong for me to want grandchildren to brighten my days?''

''Not at all. I wish you a great many.''

He patted her knee. ''Our ways are different and can be confusing, but the desires of a parent are universal. We want our children to be happy, to produce the next generation.''

''You're certainly going to get that.''

''You do not approve of Tahira.''

Billie glanced at him. ''I don't know her, but I'm sure she's a lovely young woman.''

''Then you do not understand why Jefri would enter into an arranged union.''

''I'll admit that practice is a little mind-boggling.''

''He was married before. Did he tell you?''

She nodded. ''He said she wasn't what he thought.

That she was more interested in money and position than being his wife.''

''That is correct. When Jefri learned of this, he came to me to ask for a divorce, which I granted. He was sad to see his marriage end, but not heartbroken. I realized then he had never loved her.'' The king looked into the distance. ''I have married for duty and for love, and I have learned that marrying for love is better. I tried to tell him that, but he would not listen. When it was time for him to produce heirs, he asked me to find him the proper bride.''

Billie bristled as she remembered Jefri's list. ''Docile, reasonably attractive and good with children.''

The king raised his eyebrows. ''He told you that?''

''Sometimes the prince only *looks* intelligent.''

He laughed. ''Perhaps you are correct. I waited for him to find his own bride, but he did not seem to be interested in looking, so I agreed to conduct the search myself.''

''Enter Tahira.''

''Yes. She is a good girl, raised by the sisters, instructed on how to be the right kind of wife.''

Billy couldn't help thinking of the trained animals in a circus.

''How lucky for her,'' she said, hoping the words didn't sound too sarcastic.

''You do not approve.''

''I doubt my opinion matters.''

''There are other circumstances,'' the king said. ''Her father was a close friend of mine and I promised to look after her. The school sheltered her from the world and now she has to leave.''

Billie turned to him. ''You chose the school specifically. You wanted Tahira to be innocent, raised in a manner to make her worthy of being a princess. You thought she *should* marry one of your sons.''

He nodded.

''Why not Crown Prince Murat?'' she asked in a moment of desperation.

''Tahira would not survive the rigors of being queen. She isn't strong enough.''

''Which leaves only Jefri,'' Billie said dully.

''It is a matter of honor. To break the engagement now would be to dishonor the memory of my friend and Tahira's good name.''

Of course, Billie thought. Why would anything be easy?

''Tahira could break things off,'' the king added. ''If she wanted to.''

''Right.'' Because she had so many other choices. No doubt she'd been raised expecting to marry Jefri from the time she could grasp the concept. What young woman in Tahira's place would *want* to say no?

''Still, I will not force my son into a marriage he does not want,'' the king said. ''Should Jefri come to me...''

He let the words trail away, but she had already figured out what he meant. Should Jefri go to his father and demand the engagement be broken, the king would agree. But there would be a scandal and Jefri would be seen as selfish and willful. Tahira would be dishonored and while Billie wasn't sure what went along with that, she knew it couldn't be good.

It was a lot to ask, based on one night of great sex.

"Jefri won't come to you," she said with a sureness that made the ache inside worse. "He and I..." She swallowed. "We never had a relationship. There's nothing for either of us to get over."

"As you wish, my dear."

It wasn't as she wished, but it was exactly as it was. Billie excused herself and called for Muffin. Most of the time she really liked her life, but sometimes, like now, it sucked.

Billie and Muffin walked back to their room. Billie figured she was due a long soak in the massive tub. She would use her most expensive bath salts and do her best to float away her troubles. She would stay in until she got all wrinkly, then she would put on the fluffy robe provided by the palace, curl up in bed and watch chick flicks from the DVD collection. She'd more than earned the time to lick her wounds.

But as she walked toward her door, she saw someone leaning against the wall. As her heart didn't even flicker, she knew it wasn't Jefri. Muffin gave a little bark of excitement and ran down the hallway. Her dog only ever got that happy when Doyle was around.

"What do you want?" Billie asked as she approached. "Just so you know—I'm not in the mood for a lecture."

"I wasn't planning to give one," he said as he held

her dog and fondled Muffin's ears. "I'm just checking on you."

"I'm still alive, still breathing. Is that information enough?"

One look in Doyle's blue eyes told her the answer was no. She sighed, then pushed opened the door and stood back to let him in.

"You have ten minutes," she said. "Then I want to take a bath."

Her brother set down the dog. "How bad are you hurt?" he asked.

The unexpected question, not to mention the concern in his voice, nearly did her in. Tears burned in her eyes and she had to blink them back.

"I'm fine."

"You never were much of a liar," he said, his expression grim. "Dammit, Billie, I tried to warn you."

"I'm fine," she repeated, doing her best to mean it this time. "We had a few laughs, a good time and now it's over."

Doyle narrowed his gaze. "Tell me he didn't break your heart."

She dismissed the statement with a flick of her wrist. "I didn't know him long enough for him to break anything. Come on. It was a few days. Am I happy that there's now someone else? No. But I'm not destroyed. I'll get over this and move on with my life."

She liked how the words sounded, how *she* sounded, but there was a cold place inside that told her she might not be telling the truth about any of it.

Better not to go there, she thought.

"He's a bastard," Doyle said flatly as he shoved his hands into his slacks pockets. "I should go beat the crap out of him."

"While I appreciate the sentiment, I would urge caution. There are several flaws in your plan."

"Such as?"

"Jefri isn't totally to blame. He didn't know about Tahira either."

"He sent his father looking for a wife. In my book that makes him damn guilty."

"Agreed, but he also asked him to call off the search." Billie tried to focus on the sweetness of her brother wanting to take care of her rather than the pain of Jefri's betrayal. "He was just as shocked as the rest of us."

"But you're the one who was hurt," Doyle insisted. "I should go find him right now and reduce him to mush."

"Not a good idea. Whatever the outcome, you'd probably be thrown in prison. I doubt they'd treat you very well, so I'd be forced to sell myself to the head guard just to get you food and water."

Doyle moved close and cupped her cheek. "I'm not kidding, Billie. I want him to pay."

She nodded. "I'm not kidding either. I want you to stay out of this. You're not in charge of my life."

"I told you this would happen if you got involved with him but you wouldn't listen."

She hadn't wanted to listen. She'd wanted to be

with Jefri. He'd excited her and challenged her. She'd thought...

She'd thought a lot of things, she admitted to herself. She'd wanted the fantasy—a handsome prince who adored her. Well, for twenty-four hours she'd had just that. Now it was back to the real world.

She stepped back from Doyle's touch and squared her shoulders. "I'm going to be okay with this," she said firmly. "I'm a little rattled by what happened because coming home to Jefri's fiancée seems grossly unfair, but I suppose that's the downside of dating a prince. We had a good time. I don't regret what happened and I refuse to apologize for it."

"That sounds pretty tough."

"It's the truth. You can believe it or not."

He shook his head. "This is why we've all tried to protect you. Left on your own, you get into trouble."

"It's my life, Doyle. You can't protect me forever. And while we're on the subject, let me point out at least I took a chance. When was the last time you got involved with any woman who wasn't a brainless nit? God forbid you meet a woman you can actually connect with on some level other than sex. But that would ruin it for you, wouldn't it? I don't know what you're running from or what you're afraid of, but I suggest you get yourself a little bit closer to normal before you start making accusations about me."

"You don't know what you're talking about."

"Want to bet?"

He glared at her, but she refused to back down. Doyle blinked first and turned away.

"Let me know if you change your mind about me beating him up," he grumbled as he walked to the door.

"I will. And I appreciate that you worry about me, even though you don't have to."

"You're my sister," he said gruffly.

She smiled for the first time since learning about Tahira. "I love you, too."

"This phase of the training involves teamwork," Billie said two days later.

She stood at the front of the largest classroom in the main hangar. Several diagrams covered the dry-erase board behind her. She'd been lecturing for the better part of an hour.

No one looking at her would ever guess anything was wrong, but Jefri knew. She might sound confident and strong, but she hadn't once looked at him.

"The sky gets small pretty fast when four or five fighters are covering the same territory. While you can't predict what your enemy will do next, you should be able to sense what your team is going to do. That's why we're spending so much time on the topic. I want you to develop a sixth sense about your teammates' actions and strategies. I want each of you to be able to predict what the other will do."

She continued talking, outlining how much time would be spent in simulations before they went out in jets.

"Crashing is so much simpler when we do it on a simulator," she said with a grin.

The men laughed. Billie's gaze swept around the room. For a split second, it landed on him. He sensed her instant tension before she quickly turned away.

He felt her pain, and he ached in return. He had tried to speak with her, but she avoided him. For how long? When would she allow him to explain? And if she did, what was there to say? The problem of Tahira had yet to be solved.

"All right," Billie said. "Let's go try all this theory on the simulators."

The pilots rose and followed her out of the classroom. Jefri hung back, biding his time. Even if she avoided him during the day, she still came home to the palace in the evening.

She led the first pilots through the simulation of flying together in formation. In less than three minutes he heard the sound of an explosion followed by swearing.

Billie looked up from her seat at the master control console.

"You know, this whole flying thing means we can do more than go back and forth. We can also go up and down."

The pilot who'd messed up stepped out of the simulator and grinned sheepishly. "I wasn't looking down."

"Which explains why you crashed into the plane below yours. This is not a good thing. Okay, who's next?"

The team worked through the program until they had finished. Finally only Jefri was left.

He stepped toward the simulator. Billie pushed the buttons to set the controls, then stepped aside to let him enter. Before he took his seat, he glanced at her.

"How long do you plan to avoid me?" he asked, his voice low even though they were the last two people left in the simulation room.

"Indefinitely," she said. "The computer will act as the other pilots. The program is simple—don't try to get fancy."

He'd heard the lecture before. "I know what I'm doing."

"Really?" She stared at him. "I'd have to say I don't agree with that statement."

She moved back to the main controls. "Push the start button when you're ready."

He settled himself into the seat and focused on the cockpit. The detailed simulation made it seem as if he were actually flying. After familiarizing himself with what was expected, he reached for the controls, then started the program.

He immediately found himself in the middle of an attack. There were three other planes with him and one of the enemy. One of the planes on his side signaled tone-lock.

Jefri instinctively banked left. The second the sensation of movement washed over him, he knew he'd made a mistake. He wasn't alone in the skies and—

The windshield cracked and the controls shuddered in a poor imitation of a crash.

Billie jumped out of her chair and raced over to the simulator.

"What the hell are you playing at?" she demanded in obvious fury. "How dare you fly so badly? That was barely ten seconds."

He knew she was right. Unfortunately his attention was not on his job.

"This is damned expensive equipment and my time is valuable. If you're not willing to take this seriously, then get out of here and free up some time for someone who is."

Fire flashed in her eyes. Her breath came quickly. Even in anger, she was beautiful and passionate. Need flooded him. Not just to have her with him in bed, but to simply talk and touch. There were so many things he hadn't been able to find out. They'd had too little time together.

"Well?" she asked. "Do you think this is a game?"

"Not at all."

"You lasted less than ten seconds," she pointed out again. "We both know you're better than that."

"I am sorry," he told her.

He meant for more than the simulation. She pressed her lips together.

"It doesn't matter."

"Yes, it does," he said. He reached for her hand.

She pulled back. "Don't do that. You're engaged."

"Not officially."

"It's official enough for me. Besides, there's no way you could want someone like Tahira and someone like me. We couldn't be more different."

"Who said I wanted Tahira?"

She tucked her hands behind her back. "You asked for someone like her."

"Maybe I made a mistake."

Something flickered in her eyes. Hope, he wondered. But then the emotion faded.

"You're going to have to live with that mistake," she said. "It's a matter of honor."

His mouth twisted. "You have been speaking with my father."

"He didn't tell me anything I didn't already know. You made your decision long before you met me. There's nothing either of us can do about it."

"If I could change things, would you want me to?" he asked.

She stared at him for a long time. He tried to read her thoughts, but he couldn't. Her blue eyes gave nothing away. Heat flared between them, as did wanting. He refused to believe that was only on his side. Billie had to feel it, too.

"No," she said at last, then turned to walk away.

Chapter Eleven

Billie felt as if she'd joined the cast of a popular but intense daytime drama. There was intrigue, royalty, steamy sex and a bright, young ingenue with a broken heart.

"So this is sweeps week," she murmured as she walked toward her room in the palace. She could only hope that her life would calm down over time. She didn't think she could stand this emotional pace much longer.

Her suite door beckoned. After an afternoon of simulation training, ending with that heated discussion with Jefri, all she wanted was to be left alone for the rest of the day. No more outbursts from her brother, no meetings with the king, no sensual, smoldering close encounters with Jefri. Just peace and quiet.

She opened the suite door. "It's me," she called to let Muffin know she was home.

As usual her small dog yapped in greeting, but she didn't bound over to see her. That was because Muffin was neatly curled up in Tahira's lap.

Billie stared at her uninvited guest. The young woman sat on the floor by the sofa. Several fashion magazines lay scattered around her. The one she held dropped from her hands as she quickly pushed Muffin off her, then scrambled to her feet.

"I'm so sorry," Tahira said, panic filling her eyes. "I did not mean to intrude. I waited outside, but the maid said I should come in and then your dog was so friendly and these magazines..." Tahira ducked her head and twisted her fingers together in a picture of abject misery and contrition.

Billie dropped her purse on a table and kicked off her shoes. She felt both old and weary. If she'd been a drinker, this would have been the moment to indulge. Instead she found herself wishing for a really big bowl of chocolate chip ice cream.

"It's okay," she said as she walked over to the club chair and sat down. Muffin instantly jumped on her lap.

"I intruded," Tahira said, still not looking up.

"You sat on the floor and read a few magazines. That's not exactly the same as identity theft. Really. It's fine. Have a seat."

The girl sank onto the sofa. "You are very kind."

What Billie felt the most at the moment was crabby and out of sorts. Nothing in her world was right and most of that had been caused by the teenager sitting across from her. Hard to believe that someone so quiet and shy could be the reason, yet there it was.

Tahira's long dark hair hung nearly to her waist. The heavy weight overpowered her delicate features and petite body. Billie wasn't all that tall but next to the teenager, she was practically a giant.

Jefri's fiancée had dressed in another shapeless, ugly dress. Obviously princess preparation with the nuns hadn't included classes on being a snappy dresser. Her gaze drifted down to the magazines scattered on the floor. They were all about clothes and makeup and relationships. Not exactly favorites in diplomatic circles. Had Tahira even seen a fashion magazine before?

"What did you think of those?" Billie asked, pointing at one glossy cover.

Tahira glanced at her and smiled. "They're wonderful!" she breathed. "The clothes are so amazing and the women… I could never look like that."

"Most of us couldn't," Billie said with a laugh. "We shouldn't even try. But it's fun to get ideas about clothes and that sort of thing."

Tahira fingered her moss-green dress. "I have no fashionable clothes. Not yet. At the school we dressed modestly. The sisters didn't approve of anything else."

"You're not at the school anymore."

"I know." Tahira sighed. "This palace is so different from what I grew up with. There are so many men."

"I guess they weren't allowed at the school?"

"Not at all." Tahira looked shocked at the idea. "There were priests, of course. And one of the doctors was a man, but he was very old. I met the king a few times. He was kind enough to visit me every year or so."

Billie found it difficult to imagine such a life. "What about trips? Didn't you go anywhere on vacation?"

"No." The girl shook her head. "We traveled a little on the island, but only in groups and never in the tourist season."

Sounded like prison to her, Billie thought.

She put Muffin on the floor, then collected the magazines. "I've read all of these," she said, thrusting the stack at Tahira. "You may take them if you'd like."

"Really?" Tahira's eyes brightened. "You are very kind."

Less than you might think. Billie shrugged as she resumed her seat. "It's no big deal."

The teenager hugged the magazines close. "You fly jets."

Billie laughed. "Are you asking or telling?"

"Both, I suppose. Prince Jefri mentioned it. He said you are very talented. Your work, it sounds exciting and dangerous."

"It's all I know."

"I'm afraid to fly," Tahira said in a small voice. "The plane goes so quickly and then the ground is far away. It doesn't seem right."

"It gets easier with practice."

The girl scooted to the edge of her seat. "It's not just flying," she admitted softly. "Many things frighten me. Prince Jefri, for one. He is so tall and commanding. When he speaks I think about running and hiding behind the sofa."

Billie resisted the urge to run screaming from the room. This was not a conversation she wanted to be having. Certainly not with Jefri's fiancée. But it seemed as if the girl had no one else to help her.

"There's no need to be frightened of the man you're going to marry," Billie said with a smile. "He's not that scary. Actually, he's very nice and kind."

Tahira's mouth thinned. "I never know what to say when I'm with him. Most of the time I don't say anything. He's nothing like the sisters."

Billie grinned. "I would have to agree with that. But it's a good thing."

"Maybe." She glanced around as if making sure they were alone. "I don't think he likes me very much."

Billie bit back a groan. This wasn't fair. Why her? There were other women in the palace. Cleo, Prince Sadik's wife. Or secretaries and female staff.

"You barely know him and he barely knows you," Billie said, trying to be reasonable. "You need to spend more time together to figure out if you like each other."

Tahira looked doubtful. "I thought I would know.

I thought when I finally met Prince Jefri, my heart would beat faster and my knees would get weak.''

Billie stared at the girl. ''What exactly do you know about weak knees?''

Tahira ducked her head. ''Some of the girls had families. They went home for holidays and when they came back they brought books for the rest of us. You know, stories about falling in love.'' She glanced up and bit her lower lip. ''Do you think it was wrong of me to read them?''

''Of course not.''

''I wasn't sure and there was no one to ask. So when I met Prince Jefri I thought…'' Her voice trailed off. ''Perhaps the feelings will come later. As you say, we don't know each other.''

Billie tried to be fair. Tahira seemed like a sweet enough girl, but she was no match for a stubborn, arrogant, wonderful man like Jefri. He was going to run her in circles. Not that this was her problem.

''Give it time,'' she said.

''I will,'' Tahira promised. ''I'm doing all I can to make the prince proud of me. I've been keeping up on current events so that when I attend the state dinner at the end of the week I can speak without embarrassing him.''

''Sounds like a plan.''

The state dinner, huh? Billie had been invited and until Tahira's arrival, she'd been looking forward to attending, but now she wasn't so sure.

''I don't know what to wear,'' Tahira said, then

swallowed. "My clothes from the convent, well, the sisters picked them out."

Ah, so that explained the problem.

"Now you can pick out your own," she said, going for cheerful and wondering how she could politely ask Tahira to leave. Billie felt the beginnings of a headache at her temples.

"I know nothing of fashion or even what is appropriate. I know three languages and the correct way to address every head of state, but not what to wear at a formal dinner. If I'm wrong, Prince Jefri will be disappointed."

Billie held in a groan. "I'm sure there are some stores in town that…"

"Yes," Tahira said eagerly. "The prince has told me to go shopping. I have an appointment tomorrow morning. I was hoping you would come with me."

Billie wanted to say no. Even though she loved shopping nearly as much as flying there was no way she wanted to spend an entire day with Jefri's fiancée. Even if the girl was clueless.

"I'm not an expert on dressing for the palace," she said, trying not to feel as if she were kicking a puppy.

"But you are so beautiful. And you have such style."

Billie knew there was going to be trouble if Tahira thought *she* was stylish. "I think I like sparkle a little bit more than the average princess," she said.

"No. Your clothes are perfect."

Billie knew she was being punished. Probably for giving in to Jefri in the first place. Maybe it would be easier to surrender to the inevitable and get it over with.

"Why not," she said with a sigh. "I'll go shopping with you."

Tahira's whole face lit up. "Thank you so much. You are very kind. Is ten in the morning acceptable?"

"Sure."

She would have to let Doyle know he was on his own for classes. Her brother would complain, but so what? Besides, a day spent with Tahira meant a day not spent with Jefri and right now she could use a break from his particular brand of temptation.

Billie decided to bring Muffin along for moral support. Plus her dog always loved a good shopping spree. Promptly at ten the following morning, she made her way to the main entrance of the palace where she found Tahira waiting.

The girl had traded in her ugly green dress for an ugly brown one. Her long hair had been pulled back in a plain braid and not a dot of makeup touched her skin. Billie itched to have a go at her thick eyebrows. Some plucking, a bit of eye shadow and lip gloss and the girl would be a hundred percent more attractive. She was less sure about the hair. Of course it needed cutting but in what kind of style and how long should—

"Good. You are here."

The words, spoken in a low, male voice, made her insides quiver and her thighs tremble. Still clutching

Muffin, Billie turned and saw Jefri walking toward them.

She glanced back at Tahira. "Your fiancé is coming with us?"

"Yes. When I told Prince Jefri about our outing, he wanted to join us."

Her dark eyes pleaded with Billie. Whether for Billie not to leave her alone with him or for Billie not to be angry, she wasn't sure.

Jefri stopped in front of her. "I will accompany you to the boutique."

Billie did her best not to notice how good he looked in his tailored suit and how much she wanted to step into his embrace.

"It's shopping," she said, determined to ignore her reaction. "Men hate to shop."

"I will make an exception this one time," he said, his gaze never leaving her face. "Tahira requires a complete new wardrobe, including formal wear. I will speak with the person in charge and make sure you are both well taken care of."

Of course he would, she thought as he put a hand on the small of her back and led her out of the palace. He would take charge because that is what he did—instinctively, she would bet. He would spend the day with them, always *there* so that she would be unable to think or function.

Tahira trailed after them, obviously unaware of the undercurrents swirling around. When they reached the limo, she went first, stepping in and settling on the side bench rather than the rear one. Billie followed, with Jefri sliding in after her. Which meant the two of them were sitting next to each other.

"I love your little dog," Tahira said as the car pulled away from the palace. She leaned forward and patted Muffin. "The cats are nice, too. There are so many."

"Billie is not fond of the cats," Jefri said. "They made her nervous."

Tahira looked concerned. "They won't hurt you," she said earnestly. "Most of them are very gentle. I like how they purr when I pet them."

As the girl spoke, she looked at Billie and Muffin, but never at Jefri. Apparently she hadn't been kidding when she'd said she was afraid of him. Billie wanted to tell her not to sweat it—that while he might act all high and mighty, Jefri was simply a guy. Okay, a guy with a lot of money and an incredible history, but still, he was human.

She thought about how they'd argued and laughed and how he'd never seemed to mind that she was the better pilot. If only, she thought, then shook her head. There would be no "if onlys." Not in this situation.

The boutique stood on a wide street at the edge of a large bazaar. Tahira gazed longingly at the gaudy silver bangles and lengths of embroidered cloth, but Jefri steered her into the elegant clothing shop. Billie and Muffin followed.

The store smelled of flowers, spices and money. It was just the sort of place where Billie loved to spend an afternoon and do some serious damage on her credit card. She had a feeling that today was going to be different. With Jefri around, she would need to stay on her toes and not allow herself to slip into the shopping zone.

The owner waited just inside. Tea and coffee were offered while Jefri explained their purpose. Tahira was to be provided with a new wardrobe. Billie would offer guidance.

Billie glanced down at her high-heeled sandals, skintight jeans and red leather wrap shirt. Her style leaned toward gaudy and fun. Tahira was destined to be an actual princess. Maybe it would be better to keep her advice-giving to a minimum.

"You must allow me to thank you for your kindness in this matter," Jefri said when Tahira had been led away to the dressing rooms.

Billie set down Muffin. When she straightened, she was careful to keep her distance from Jefri. "No thanks are necessary."

She plucked a black lace blouse off a rack and winced when she saw the twelve hundred dollar price tag. Talk about pricey.

"I want you to pick out whatever you would like," he said.

She put the blouse back and drew in a deep breath. "I don't need your money. I can afford my own clothes."

"I know you can. I am trying to…"

She looked at him. "Yes? Trying to what?"

He glared at her. "You make a difficult situation impossible."

"Me? What did I do?"

"You stand there, taunting me."

Billie glanced over her shoulder to make sure he wasn't talking to anyone else. "I'm not taunting you."

"You tempt me with every breath. And now, when I try to offer something insignificant and make a gesture, you throw it back in my face."

What? Were they having separate conversations here?

"What gesture? The clothes?"

"Yes. I cannot say how I feel. I cannot offer you gifts, except like this."

A dilemma fit for a prince, Billie thought, not sure how to react. "Look, I'm okay with all this." Not really, but what else could she say? "I don't need—"

He touched her arm. The light contact barely grazed her leather shirt, but she felt it down to her bones. The world around them seemed to disappear. There was only the moment and the man and what could have been.

"Please," he breathed.

"It's just clothes," she told him.

"Is it?"

She didn't understand the question, but in the end it was easier to simply shrug and say, "If it means that much to you."

"It does."

The owner returned then. She was a tall, white-haired woman who had the elegant European bone structure.

"Tahira will begin with casual clothing. Come, child."

Tahira appeared in an elegant pantsuit. The tailored jacket emphasized modest curves, while the cut of the pants made her legs look longer.

"Very nice," Billie said with a genuine smile. "Do you like it?"

The girl hesitated, then glanced at Jefri. "What do *you* think?"

He nodded.

Tahira beamed. "Then I like it, too." She walked back to the dressing room.

Billie managed to keep from rolling her eyes. "She is far too worshipful. You must really like that."

He frowned at her. "I do not need my ego stroked by a child."

"Too bad, because that's what you signed up for. Next time you're ordering a bride, you might want to specify an age range."

His eyes narrowed. "There will be no 'next time.' Requesting an arranged marriage was madness."

Too bad he'd figured that out too late, she thought glumly.

"She's a baby," she reminded him. "You can't hurt her."

"So now you take her side?"

"Someone has to. I mean it, Jefri. You are her entire world."

He stared into her eyes. "That is not what I wanted."

"It's what you got and now you're stuck."

As was she. She glanced around on the pretense of looking for Muffin. ''I need to go find my dog,'' she said and hurried away.

She wouldn't care, she told herself. Not about him. Not about what could have been. There was no future here. When the contract was up, she would get in her plane and fly away without once looking back. There was no alternative.

The morning crawled by. Jefri had not considered the torture of being confined with Billie in the small area of the shop and having to pretend she didn't matter. He couldn't touch her or have her close to him. He had to keep his attention on Tahira, enduring her overeager smiles and attempts to please him. The girl had no opinions of her own, no thoughts, save his. He supposed he should have enjoyed that, but he did not.

Billie kept carefully out of reach, as elusive as a beam of light. She disappeared on the pretext of looking for a certain dress, or getting another size for Tahira, or finding her dog. As Muffin had curled up on a cushion on the floor and gone to sleep, the latter excuse was the most feeble, but a part of him understood why she felt the need to pretend.

Tahira appeared in a light green dress that skimmed her knees. The silky fabric clung to her body. In her own youthful way, she was attractive, he thought, as disconnected from her as if he viewed a sculpture. She was reasonably intelligent and gentle of spirit. Her only sin was to not be the woman who haunted his dreams.

"What do *you* think?" he asked before she could request his opinion.

Tahira blinked at him. "But you are the prince."

"So I have been told. You have not answered my question."

She looked confused, as if her opinion had never been requested. Carefully, she faced the mirror and studied herself.

"The color is good," she said slowly. "The length does not suit me. The hem should be an inch or two shorter or longer. Some fullness here," she touched her hips "would soften the silhouette."

"As you wish," he said.

She met his gaze in the mirror. "What do you mean?"

"Have the dress altered or find another that suits you better."

Her eyes widened. "But you did not say what you thought."

"I know."

Tahira looked as out of place and frightened as a wild rabbit. She darted back to the dressing room.

"You need to pace yourself," Billie said as she appeared from around a rack of dresses. "Too much freedom all at once will only terrify her."

"So I see."

She fingered an evening gown without looking at it. "I'm glad you're going to be kind to her."

"Is there another choice?"

"Of course, but I like that you don't think so."

"You have yet to try on clothing."

She shrugged. "This place isn't exactly my kind of store."

"Why do I know that is not true?" She walked around the rack of dresses and he followed. "There must be something that tempts you."

When she didn't answer, he began to study the evening gowns. They were all elegant and formal, but nothing about them caught his eye until he saw a beaded dress. The various shades of blue were as beautiful as the Arabian Sea. They swirled across the fabric in a glittering pattern that dazzled the eye.

"This one," he said, pulling it out and handing it to her.

"No, I couldn't," she said automatically, even as her fingers rubbed the delicate fabric.

He took the dress off the rack and handed it her. "Of course you could."

She took it and held it up against her. Her blue eyes darkened to the color of sapphires. "It's more of a princess dress, which isn't exactly me."

He stared at her, wanting what he could not have and unable to want what he could.

"Try it on," he insisted.

She gave in with a little nod and disappeared into the dressing area.

Jefri sank down in one of the chairs provided. He studied the way Muffin curled up on her cushion and the fabric of the carpet. In desperation, he reached for the newspaper lying on a small table. Anything to keep from imagining what Billie was doing right that moment—how she would have to undress down to just her panties before pulling on the dress and how she would look as she stood there nearly naked.

Wanting poured through him. Need grew until it overwhelmed him. Desperation propelled him to his feet. He had the thought that he would follow her into the small dressing area and claim her as his own.

Would she resist his touch? Would she yield? He knew how she would look, the texture of her skin and the scent of her body. He knew how he could carry her away on a wave of pleasure that left her boneless with contentment. He knew his own reaction to claiming her as his own.

"Prince Jefri?"

Tahira's small voice drew him back to reality. He opened his eyes and looked at the young woman in the simple black gown. The heavy fabric overwhelmed her small frame and made her seem like a girl playing dress-up.

Before he could speak, Billie appeared next to her. The shimmering fabric hugged every curve, as if the gown had been made for her. The light reflecting on the beads made her skin glow. She was a goddess next to a mortal.

Tahira stared at her reflection in the mirror and knew the dress was all wrong. It didn't hang right and there was something about the fabric itself. But what, exactly, eluded her.

She held in a sigh of frustration. If only the sisters had spent a little bit of time helping her learn how to dress instead of insisting she learn so much about geology or physics, she would be better able to handle her new position as Jefri's fiancée. So far the prince hadn't asked her a single question about rock formations.

Billie said something to the prince and he laughed. Tahira liked the sound of his laughter, even if she couldn't think of anything funny to say. But Billie always knew exactly what to say and how to act. She was perfect.

Tahira eyed her friend and the blue dress she wore. It was stunning. Jefri moved behind them both and placed a hand on each of their shoulders. While Billie smiled, Tahira stood there, frozen, the hand a lead weight on her skin.

She told herself to relax—that this was the man she would marry. But somehow she couldn't ever picture herself and the prince being together as a couple. When he talked to her, she didn't know how to answer. When they were alone, she felt only awkward and afraid. None of that seemed like love to her.

But he had honored her with his desire to claim her as his wife and she knew she had no choice but to go through with the union.

Chapter Twelve

"Everything is so beautiful," Tahira said enthusiastically as she opened box after box of clothing. "You have been more than generous." She turned around. "I am not worthy."

Jefri stood in the center of the suite and watched concern tighten the girl's expression. He forced himself to smile.

"You are more than worthy. These clothes are necessary. The sisters have many wonderful qualities, but they did not provide you an excessive wardrobe."

Tahira flashed a smile. "I was thinking the same thing at the store. How helpful is it that I can discuss quantum mechanics when I don't know what shoes to wear with what dress?"

She raced to the rack containing her formal gowns and reached for the first garment bag.

''What shall I wear Friday, Prince Jefri?'' she asked as she pulled down the zipper. ''It will be my first state dinner. I want to dress correctly.''

He appreciated her enthusiasm, even as it made him feel old and out of place.

''The black one?'' she asked. ''Not the red. That is too sophisticated, I think. There is that lovely green one…''

She continued to chatter, but he didn't listen. Instead he prowled the confines of the living room and wished he could be somewhere else.

He crossed to the French doors and stared out at the gardens below. A woman walked along a path and for a moment, he thought it was Billie. His heart jumped until he recognized his sister-in-law. No. Not Billie.

''I've never had my nails done before,'' Tahira was saying. ''Billie mentioned my hair. That I need to get it cut. What do you think?''

He looked at the young woman standing by the pile of white and gold boxes. ''Would you prefer it shorter?''

''I don't know.'' She fingered her long braid. ''Shouldn't you decide?''

She asked the question like a child and he did not want to be her father.

''No, Tahira,'' he said gently. ''The choice is yours.''

''But…''

She looked confused, as if such freedom had not occurred to her.

"You are no longer at the school," he told her. "You are free to do as you wish with your life. You may be as you choose."

Free to walk away from him, he thought, knowing she would not.

"You mean like a career?" she asked. "But we are to be married."

"The wedding could wait a while." Forever?

"Oh." She sat down on the sofa as if the thought was too much for her. "I have no idea what I would want to do. Not flying, like Billie. The thought terrifies me." She smiled. "I have trouble imagining her in a jet. She's so feminine and pretty all the time. I love her hair. The curls are perfect and I like the way she does her makeup. I wonder why she never married."

"Perhaps she never met the right man."

"I suppose. Or maybe she doesn't need to be taken care of all the time. She's independent. I wish I could be like that."

As soon as Tahira spoke the words, she covered her mouth with her hand and stared at him. Panic made her tremble.

"Prince Jefri," she began in a hushed tone.

He stopped her with a shake of his head. "You do not need to apologize, child. There is nothing wrong in wanting to be independent."

She swallowed and dropped her hand back to her lap. "But you have honored me by wanting to marry me. I can't forget that. Not ever. I swear, I will do my best to be a good and dutiful wife. You have my word.''

Not exactly what he wanted to hear.

He crossed to the sofa and pushed aside several boxes so he could sit next to her. For the first time since meeting her, he took her hands in his.

''Tahira, you must listen to me. You have been raised believing you have only one destiny and that is to marry me. But the choice is completely yours. You are free to choose another life. Should you decide you do not want to marry me, I will understand and support your decision in any way I can. You are young and it is a difficult and permanent choice.''

Her fingers moved against him. Her skin was warm and she smelled of flowers. Yet he felt nothing. Her youthful beauty left him unmoved.

Her dark gaze settled on his face. ''You are kindness itself,'' she said fiercely. ''Your goodness only convinces me that marriage is the right choice.''

He held in a groan. ''As you wish,'' he said, releasing her and rising to his feet.

She stood as well and clasped her hands together in front of her chest. ''Prince Jefri, I will do all I can to make you happy. I will be the most dutiful wife ever. I swear.''

''Of course you will, child. I have no doubt.''

He nodded, then walked to the door. With Tahira, he would get exactly what he had asked for. That was the hell of it.

Billie figured it was a good news, bad news situation. On the plus side, she was attending her first ever formal state dinner as a special invited guest of the king. She had on a killer dress and looked fabulous. Her date looked nearly as good in a carefully tailored tuxedo. The downside was that her date was her brother Doyle and that she would have to spend the evening watching Jefri pay attention to Tahira.

She reminded herself that the option was staying in her room with Muffin and watching movies. As she figured she could deal with the emotional angst of her situation on her own time and that this evening was a once-in-a-lifetime event, she'd put on her brand-new fancy dress and prepared to dance the night away.

She and Doyle followed the sound of conversation down the long corridor on the first floor and entered the massive ballroom. Dozens of chandeliers hung from a thirty-foot ceiling and illuminated the vast space and chatting guests. An orchestra sat at one end of the room. There were small tables and chairs, several strategically placed bars and waiters circulating with food and champagne.

Doyle gave a low whistle. "This is just the meet and greet, right? There's a dinner that follows, then dancing?"

"That's what the invitation said."

"All right." He scanned the room. "Lots of beautiful women. I think I'd like to be the king."

Billie gave his arm a warning squeeze. "Do your best not to embarrass me."

"Cross my heart." He kissed her cheek. "Stay away from royalty."

''You got that right.''

He grinned and sauntered off, only to be immediately claimed by a dark-haired woman in a very low-cut dress.

''The boy always seems to fall on his feet,'' Billie murmured as she turned in a slow circle.

She spotted a waiter with a tray of what looked like champagne glasses, but before she could flag him down, she sensed something hot and tempting trickle down her spine. She clenched her muscles in anticipation. Seconds later, she heard Jefri's voice.

''Good evening,'' he said, coming up behind her and offering her a full glass of bubbling champagne. ''You look exceptionally beautiful.''

''Thank you.'' She clutched the glass with both hands because the alternative was reaching for him and that wasn't allowed. Instead, she let her gaze roam over him, taking in the tuxedo, the dark and smoldering gaze.

''Where's Tahira?'' she asked.

''Speaking with a friend. Someone she knew from school is here and they are catching up. And Doyle?''

Billie motioned to the crowd. ''I'm sure he's either being seduced or is seducing someone even as we speak. He looks good in a tux and women always appreciate that.''

Jefri took her arm and led her to the side of the room. She told herself not to go, to plant herself in one very public place and refuse to have anything to do with him, but she couldn't seem to resist. Not when he looked at her as if she were the answer to all his prayers.

"What are you thinking?" he asked when they stopped in a shallow alcove.

"That we have to stop running into each other."

He left his hand on her arm and began to rub his thumb against her bare skin. "That is not what I was thinking. I want to thank you for helping Tahira with the shopping."

"She's very nice."

"Yes. She is all that I asked for. I could not be more miserable."

She flinched. "Jefri, don't. She's—"

"A child and no more interested in me than I am in her. This is a matter of circumstances. A twist of fate that must be untwisted."

"Are you going to break off the engagement? Let her go?"

Instead of answering her, he moved close. So close that she could feel the heat of him. His body brushed against hers in a gesture that claimed as well as enticed.

"I want you," he breathed into her ear. "Every moment, with every heartbeat. I think of you in my bed. Naked. I want to touch you and hold you. I want to taste you and excite you. I want you wet, aroused, screaming."

His hand moved from her arm to her stomach where he pressed his palm against her. "Do you remember what it was like?" he asked softly.

She couldn't speak or move. It was all she could

do to keep standing. "Of course," she whispered. "I can't forget, but that doesn't mean anything."

"It means the world."

She met his gaze and allowed herself to get lost there. For a moment or two, she imagined the possibilities, what could have been if things were different.

"I can't," she said and stepped away from him. "You can't either."

His gaze sharpened. "I am Prince Jefri of Bahania."

"Exactly. If you were someone else, this never would have happened. Tahira would be engaged to someone else and we…" She wasn't sure what they would be, but it wouldn't be this.

"Billie, I want you."

And she wanted him. She supposed that's what it came down to. A problem with no resolution.

"I should go," she said.

"No. Do not leave the party."

She stared at her glass. "I meant the country. This would be easier if I weren't here."

"You would quit?"

"It would make our lives go more smoothly."

"Is that what you want?"

Five simple words, she thought sadly. A question she couldn't answer. Not if she told the truth. Because she didn't want to go.

She pushed past him and entered the crowd in the ballroom. Maybe if she just kept moving, she could leave all this behind and simply have a good time.

She walked around a large woman in black satin and nearly ran into a well-dressed older man.

"I'm sorry," she began before she recognized the king.

He took her hand and patted it. "Where are you off to in such a hurry?"

"Nowhere. Just walking."

"I see. Then if I'm not taking you away from anything too important, there are some people I would like you to meet."

Billie nearly stumbled in surprise. "Me? Who?"

"The French ambassador is here. A very impressive woman. And the British prime minister. You haven't met him, have you?"

Billie laughed. "Gee, I haven't. Shocking but true."

The king drew her close. "He will be charmed, my dear. Perfectly charmed."

Tahira hovered behind a large column and watched the dancing. She had survived her first formal dinner, which was more than she'd hoped for. For the past three nights she'd had nightmares about spilling, dropping or saying the wrong thing. She'd awakened sweaty and trembling, unable to get back to sleep for hours.

Now the dinner was behind her and the worst that had happened was she had bored the people sitting around her.

"Perhaps not too great a sin," she murmured to herself as she swayed in time with the music.

The king of El Bahar had been seated on her left and while he had been most kind, he had been far more interested in his lovely wife who had been seated across from him. The Spanish ambassador had been on her right. She spoke enough of the language to get by but when he'd started talking about the wines his country exported, all she'd been able to do was nod as if she knew what he was saying. She tried not to imagine the look on his face if she'd admitted she'd never had Spanish wine, or any wine until that very night.

Several different ones had been served at dinner. She'd tried them all and had been careful to only take a sip or two. She hadn't wanted to get tipsy. Not that she would know what tipsy felt like.

A flash of blue caught her eye. She smiled when she recognized Billie dancing with the crown prince.

So beautiful, Tahira thought with a sigh. Billie had piled her blond hair up on her head. Long, dangly diamond earrings fell nearly to her shoulders, while her beaded blue dress hugged all her curves.

Tahira thought of her own small breasts and boyish hips. If someone put a dress like that on her, it would simply fall to the ground.

As she watched, the crown prince said something and Billie laughed. Tahira smiled as if she shared the joke. Billie always knew the right thing to say. She'd heard plenty of laughter at that end of the table.

"I want to be more like her," she said fiercely, wondering if it were possible. Could a mouse be transformed into a beautiful and exotic bird?

''More like who?''

Tahira spun toward the voice and saw a man standing behind her. Her mind went blank for a second before she recognized Billie's brother Doyle.

''You frightened me,'' she admitted, pressing a hand to her throat.

''Sorry. I saw you hiding back here and I came to find out why you're not dancing.''

Dancing? She winced at the thought. While she had taken lessons and practiced several times a week with the other girls at the school, she had found out during her one awkward dance with Prince Jefri that dancing with her friends was very different from dancing with a man.

''I have danced,'' she said. ''Once.''

''Let me guess. With your fiancé. But not with anyone else.''

She shook her head. ''No one has asked and I'm not sure...''

Before she could complete her thought, Doyle grabbed her hand and pulled her close.

''You're not married yet, right? So I won't be beheaded for taking you out on the floor.''

His eyes were the most amazing shade of blue, she thought hazily. Like the sea by the coral reefs off the island. A deep blue that called to her and whispered secrets.

''Tahira?''

''What?''

He grinned and her heart flipped in her chest.

''You didn't answer my question.''

She blinked. "What did you want to know?"

"Are beautiful princesses-to-be allowed to dance with handsome strangers?"

She laughed, then felt herself blush. She wasn't beautiful, but he was kind to say so.

"You're not a stranger," she said. "You're Billie's brother."

"You say that as if it makes me safe."

"It does."

His expression darkened. "Don't believe that for a moment, princess. I can be very dangerous."

His words made her shiver, but with excitement rather than fear. "I'm not a princess."

"But you will be."

For once she didn't want to think about that. "In time. But for now I am simply a girl."

"Not a woman?"

She blushed again and ducked her head.

He touched her chin. "Sorry. I didn't mean to make you uncomfortable. Come on. Dance with me."

Before she could answer, he pulled her into his embrace. His arms came around her and then they were moving to the music.

Tahira didn't know what to think, what to feel. No man had ever held her quite so close. Well, except for Prince Jefri. But he'd held her stiffly, while Doyle pulled her against him. They touched everywhere. One hand rested low on her back while the other claimed her fingers.

He was tall, but not too tall. She liked how strong he was and how she felt tiny by comparison.

"You're thinking too much," Doyle complained with a smile. "I can hear your brain working. Which is disappointing. You're supposed to be so swept away by my charms that you can't think of anything but me."

"How do you know I wasn't thinking of you?" she asked and was delighted when he laughed.

"Miss Tahira, no one told me you were a flirt. Did they teach you that at your convent school?"

Her? Flirting? Was it possible?

"Not at all," she admitted. "The sisters would not have approved."

He lowered his head until his lips were very close to her ear. "They don't need to know."

His breath made her shiver. Deep inside her chest, a funny little feeling began to grow.

This was nice, she thought. More than nice.

Doyle pulled her even closer. "You smell good. What's the name of your perfume?"

She looked at him. "I'm not wearing any."

In less than a heartbeat, his expression changed. Something dark flashed through his eyes.

"Don't tell me that, Princess," he said, his voice low and almost angry.

"I don't understand. What's wrong with me not wearing perfume?"

"No woman should smell that good on her own."

"Oh."

She had no idea what he was talking about. Was he angry? Talking to men was more confusing than she had ever imagined. When she was with Jefri she had to search her mind for something to say. With Doyle, she didn't worry so much, but she was still confused about the outcome.

They danced together in silence for a few minutes before he said, "So you're really going to marry him."

"What?"

She looked up and saw Prince Jefri dance by. She turned her head so she couldn't see him.

"Of course. He does me a great honor by requesting my hand in marriage."

"Uh-huh. Has he?"

She glanced at Doyle. "Has he what?"

"Proposed. You know, down on one knee, vowing to love and honor 'til death do you part."

"Oh. No. Not like that."

He hadn't said anything, really. One morning the sisters had come in and told her it was time to leave. So she'd packed her things and had been brought to the palace.

"The king told me," she said.

"That's romantic."

"Ours is a marriage of arrangement. I had hoped, of course, that I would be offered to one of the princes, but I didn't dare dream it would really happen."

Doyle stared at her. "Tahira, you're not a commodity. You don't have to wait around to be offered to someone."

"Why are you angry?"

"I'm not. I just don't understand how someone like you can sell herself so short."

"Someone like me?"

"You're sweet and funny. Pretty as hell. It's annoying that you're so damned honored to be given to someone like him. You could have a whole lot more."

Several things distracted her. First, Doyle's energy. He obviously cared, which surprised her and pleased her. Also, he'd sworn. She wasn't sure she'd ever heard anyone use actual swear words before. Last, but certainly not least, were his words themselves.

"He's a prince," she said. "How could I do better?"

"You could marry someone you love."

Love? "But I *will* love him. In time."

"How do you know?"

No one had ever asked her that before. "I just do."

It had always been that way. All her life she had known there was a chance she would marry one of the king's sons. To that end she had studied and prepared, always hoping. Yes, at first she and her husband would be strangers, but in time, they would fall in love.

"It's the way things are," she insisted.

The music slowed and Doyle led her off the floor. "Life isn't that tidy. You're banking your whole life on something that may or may not happen. Wouldn't you rather fall in love with someone first and *then* marry him? Or maybe you don't have to get married at all. What about that? You could explore the world. Get a job. Live."

He made it all sound possible, when she knew it wasn't. "I'm going to marry Prince Jefri."

"Why?"

"Because I have to."

As soon as the words were out, she wanted to call them back. She covered her mouth with her hands and stared at him.

"No, you don't," he said quietly.

Her eyes began to burn. "You don't understand," she said as she lowered her hand to her side.

"Actually, I do. Come. Dance with me again."

She started to move away, but then he took her hand and she found herself being led back to the floor.

Had to, want to, what did it mean? She *wanted* to marry Prince Jefri. She'd wanted it all her life.

"Stop thinking," Doyle whispered against her ear.

He pulled her closer. She let herself relax against him. Gradually her mind stilled and there was only the music and the man.

Jefri stood in the shadows and watched Tahira dance again with Doyle. They'd been together nearly an hour. He tried to find some measure of jealousy within him, but he could not. All he felt was guilt every time the girl laughed.

She never laughed around him, never smiled, barely spoke. He knew the fault lay with him. Had he tried to draw her out or tease her? Had he worked to make her smile? Of course not—he'd been too busy blaming her for not being Billie.

Speaking of which...he turned his attention from

Tahira, to the woman who occupied his mind. She danced with the British prime minister. As he watched, the older man threw back his head and laughed.

Jefri's reaction was as quick as it was powerful. He wanted to stalk across the room and rip her from the other man's arms. He wanted to insist that no one dance with her, speak with her, touch her. Only he should be allowed such privileges. Yet he could not. He was bound to another.

He looked between the two women. So different, he thought. They had nothing in common save their gender. Given the choice...

But there was no choice. Once he'd asked his father to find him a bride and his father had chosen Tahira, events had been set in motion. Events that could not be changed, regardless of his own needs and feelings. What was desire in the face of honor? He was a prince and a sheik. If his word had no value, who and what could he be?

Chapter Thirteen

"I hadn't thought I could design my own clothes," Tahira said as she laid out a length of fabric. "When Billie mentioned it, I didn't even know where to begin, but the sisters taught me to sew years ago, so I know the basics. In my trips to the bazaar, I've been able to pick up some wonderful lengths of cloth."

She smiled. "What do you think of this one?"

Jefri glanced down at the fabric draped across the coffee table. Thin lines of gold shot through the deep red material.

"It's very nice," he said, not knowing what else to tell her.

Tahira's smile faded. "You don't like it."

"I have no opinion. If you like it, then make something." He tried to sound kind and interested, even though he hadn't been listening to much of what she'd said.

"But if you don't approve." Her mouth twisted. "You think my hobby is foolish."

"Not at all." Boring, maybe, but not foolish. "Tahira, whatever delights you delights me."

"Billie said it was important for me to find some interests," she told him. "Things that would occupy my time. You're so busy with your responsibilities. Not that I'm complaining, of course. I would never complain."

"I know that, child."

Tahira would never complain, never speak out against anything he might want to do. She was obedient, soft-spoken and kind. In the past month since the ball and his realization that he had no choice but to keep his word, Jefri had made a serious effort to get to know her. She was all he could have asked for and nothing he wanted. Worse, Billie had befriended her so every time he was with Tahira all the girl talked about, aside from clothes, design and fabric, was Billie.

"I'm glad you are settling in and finding things that bring you pleasure."

Her eyes widened and she looked away. "I'm only interested in pleasing you, Prince Jefri."

"Of course."

"Is there something else you require of me?"

"No."

She reached for another bolt of cloth and began to explain what she would use it for. While he tried to listen, his mind drifted to his flight training that morning. He'd lasted all of four minutes against Billie. When they'd met up again on the tarmac, she'd given him a quick smile of congratulation.

"You're doing great," she'd told him.

"I thought I'd get good enough to beat you," he'd admitted.

"No one gets that good."

She'd grinned then, and he laughed and for that moment in time, the world had been right. Then she'd turned away as if she didn't know him. As if they had never been lovers.

He understood her need to withdraw. The pain of wanting and not having was too great. But even though he respected her decision and agreed with it, for him, nothing had changed. He still ached when he saw her. He still dreamed about her. He could still pick her out in a crowd simply by the delicate scent of her skin. He listened to the rapid click of her high heels in the hallway and had even taken to seeking out Muffin knowing that Billie was always near her dog.

There were nights when he decided he would simply take her and disappear. He told himself they could find refuge in the desert, living out quiet, happy lives away from the real world. Except he knew he could not claim to care about her if he also sought to clip her wings. Billie had been born to fly.

Which left him trapped in circumstances that seemed intolerable.

"You will excuse me," he said, cutting Tahira off in midsentence.

She blinked in surprise. "Yes. Of course."

He walked out of her suite and headed for the business wing of the palace. He ached in a way he wouldn't have thought possible, and knew the pain would never go away. When Billie left Bahania, she would take his heart with her. Such a thing could not be allowed.

The guards outside the large carved doors nodded as he approached. Jefri stopped in front of the desk inside.

"Is my father in?" he asked the forty-something male assistant.

"Of course. I'll let him know you're here."

Jefri was announced and stepped into his father's large office.

The king of Bahania sat on an old sofa by the window. Several cats lay around the room. Two curled up on different chairs, while one had stretched out in a spot of sun on a bookcase. Jefri picked up a gray short-haired cat and set it on the ground, then brushed off the cushion and took its place.

"This is a surprise," the king said cheerfully. "I assume you have no crisis to report? The air force still flies?"

"Yes, Father. We have improved greatly. The Van Horns have done an excellent job."

"Good. They have lived up to their reputation." His father leaned back in the sofa and smiled. "What can I do for you, my son?"

Jefri drew in a deep breath. "I cannot marry Tahira, Father. I have tried. For the past month I have spent time with her, learning about her. We have taken walks, long drives, spent afternoons picnicking by the sea. She is a lovely young woman with all the qualities I requested."

The king frowned. "Then what is the problem?"

"I cannot care about her. I am in love with someone else."

His father patted the cat on his lap. "I see," he said at last. "And that young woman would be?"

"Billie."

"Ah."

Jefri couldn't tell what his father thought by his expression or the tone of his voice. Perhaps he should explain more.

"I do not believe it is within my power to make Tahira happy," he said. "She needs someone who will see her for herself, and not for what she can never be. I will do whatever I must—settle money on her, send her to college. I want her happiness more than anything."

"Have you discussed this with her?" the king asked.

"Not yet."

"What if she decides her happiness lies with you?"

"Then she is mistaken."

His father glanced at him. "She has lived in the palace for nearly six weeks. People have noticed, speculated. If you were to cast her aside now..."

"She is not being cast aside," Jefri insisted. "There has been no formal engagement."

"Tahira has considered no life except that as your wife. Promises were made. Will she not see this past month as courtship?"

Jefri stared out the window. Of course she would. How else could Tahira interpret events?

"She does not love me," he said.

"How do you know? Have you asked? Are you going to break this girl's heart and destroy her life? She is only here because you asked for her."

Jefri felt sure his father wanted to tell him something, but that he would not speak outright. So what was the clue? Something about Tahira. Did the girl love him? She could not. Surely she saw how wrong they were for each other. Or did she expect so little that an unhappy arrangement was enough?

Too many questions, he thought in frustration.

"This cannot be," he told his father.

"This must be," the king said.

Jefri rose to his feet. "I will find another way."

His father said nothing as he stalked out of the room.

The king watched his youngest son leave. When the door had closed, he smiled.

"It is safe. You can come out now."

Something moved under the wing chair. Two small brown eyes glanced around cautiously.

"He is gone," the king said, then patted the space next to him on the sofa.

Muffin jumped up and cuddled close. The king stroked her back.

"You see," he said. "Everything is going according to plan. It is just a matter of time until we have exactly what we both want."

Tahira sat in the garden, doing her best not to cry. But it seemed the harder she tried not to, the more her eyes burned.

Something was very wrong. Somehow she had displeased Prince Jefri. But what had she said or done? All she thought about was what she could do to make him happy. She listened dutifully as he talked about flying and jets, even though all the technical information made her head ache. She did her best to enjoy all their visits to museums and parks. She had asked several times and he always said he didn't mind that she was spending her free time designing clothes.

So why were things between them even more strained than they had been at the beginning? And why had he spent the past two days avoiding her?

"Beautiful women shouldn't cry."

Tahira jumped when she heard the words. She turned on the stone seat and saw Doyle walking toward her.

She hadn't seen him in nearly two weeks, and that one encounter had been a brief conversation at a family dinner. Even knowing it was wrong, she couldn't help being delighted to see him now and she hoped he would have time to talk with her.

"I'm not crying," she said even as she wiped away the tears that had trickled down her cheek.

Doyle sat next to her on the bench. "What could possibly make you so sad?" he asked.

"Nothing. I'm fine." Now.

She looked at his handsome face, the easy smile that always made her lips curve up in return. She wanted to get lost in his dark blue eyes and never find her way back.

"So how's my favorite princess?" he asked as he took her hand in his.

"I'm not a princess," she said, trying to tug her fingers free.

He didn't let go.

She glanced around to make sure they were alone. She could not be seen holding hands with a man other than Prince Jefri. Not that the prince had ever tried to. When she realized they were in a secluded part of the garden, she allowed herself to relax and enjoy the warm touch of Doyle's skin against hers.

"So what's the problem?" he asked as he brought her knuckles to his mouth and kissed them.

She felt the warm contact clear down to her toes. He'd kissed her hand! Just like that. While talking! As if... As if...

She couldn't even think. No one had ever done that. Of course no one had ever kissed her anywhere before.

Why? Why had Doyle done that and why had the contact made her tingle?

"W-what was the question?" she asked.

He grinned. "Why are you hiding out in the garden and trying not to cry?"

"Oh. That."

She pulled her hand free of his embrace and held in a sigh. "Prince Jefri doesn't like me very much."

"Huh. That doesn't sound good, what with you two practically engaged."

She stared at him. "What do you mean, practically?"

"Has he proposed?"

"Well, no."

"Are you wearing a ring?"

She glanced at her left hand. "No."

"In my world, that means you're not completely engaged. Is it different here?"

Tahira hadn't thought of it that way. "But there is an understanding. I was raised to marry a prince. Jefri asked for his father to arrange a match." Her shoulders slumped. "I fear he is disappointed in me."

"No way."

"It's true. We have nothing to talk about. Things aren't very comfortable." She wanted to mention that the prince had never once held her hand or tried to kiss her, but she couldn't bring herself to admit that to Doyle.

"You don't have a lot of experience with the boy-girl thing," he told her. "Maybe you're making things out to be worse than they are."

She didn't think so. "I was too sheltered," she said. "I wish I were more like your sister. Billie has a career and accomplishments. She's so confident."

"She's okay," Doyle said. "Why can't you have a career if you want one?"

"Because."

"There's an answer."

Tahira didn't know what else to say. "I would have to go to college."

"So?"

"But that would never be allowed."

"Why not?"

Two simple words. Two words with the power to alter the very fabric of her world.

Could she? Was she allowed to express preferences and make choices?

"I was raised to marry a prince," she repeated.

"Times change. It's a new century, kid, and you can be a whole lot more than some guy's possession if that's what you want."

She didn't know what to think. The possibilities overwhelmed her.

"I never thought…"

"Then it's time to start thinking." He grinned. "I do have to warn you, though. Once you leave the palace, it's a big, bad world out there and guys like me are going to want to eat you up for breakfast."

She frowned. "What?"

He leaned close. "I'm talking about men, Princess."

She ignored the title. "What about them?"

"They're going to want you."

As in… She wasn't sure as in what, but it sounded exciting. "I don't think Prince Jefri wants me."

"Then he's an idiot."

She gasped. "You can't say that about a prince."

"Sure I can. I'll say it again. He's an idiot."

Then, before she could think or catch her breath or figure out what was happening, Doyle leaned close and brushed his mouth against hers.

Tahira couldn't believe it. He'd kissed her! Just like that. With no warning or anything. Just a quick, fabulous, amazing touch.

"You look stunned," he said, sounding faintly amused.

"I am."

"Let me guess. No one's done that before."

"The king kisses my cheek."

"Not the same." Doyle shifted closer, then cupped her chin. "We're going to try it again. This time, close your eyes."

"Why?"

"Because I said so."

"Oh. All right." She obediently closed her eyes.

He chuckled. "Why do I know you're going to get headstrong in a hurry?"

"I have no idea. How long do I keep my eyes closed?"

"As long as you want."

A soft puff of breath was her only warning, then his mouth was on hers again, but this time it was much more than a brush. His lips pressed against hers in a way that made her blood heat and her fingers curl into her palms. She practically squirmed in her seat as her brain tried to process all the bits of information.

Like how softly he kissed her, yet how firm his lips were. How she could feel the heat from his body surrounding her like a blanket and how her skin felt extra sensitive.

He shifted, dropping the hand that had been cupping her chin to her waist. She felt his individual fingers and the way he squeezed her.

He drew back. "Put your hands on my shoulders."

She opened her eyes and stared at him. "We shouldn't be doing this."

"Because of the prince?"

She nodded.

"Let him get his own girl."

"I *am* his girl."

"Not until I see a ring. Now either put your hands on my shoulders and brace yourself for another kiss or run back inside like a good princess-to-be."

Tahira stared at him. The choice was very clear. The part of her telling her to run seemed to be getting more and more quiet while the part of her that wanted to keep on kissing Doyle got louder and louder.

Slowly, tentatively, she raised her arms until she could rest her hands on his shoulders. He was big and muscular and solid. She liked that. She liked a lot of things.

"What did you think about the kissing?" he asked.

She ducked her head and blushed. "It was very nice."

"Ready for more?"

She nodded.

"Ever hear of French kissing?"

Her breath stuck in her throat. Of course she had. In books. And sometimes other girls talked. About how a boy...or in Doyle's case, a man...would put his tongue... They would kiss with...

"Tahira, look at me."

She forced herself to raise her head and meet his gaze. The kindness there eased her embarrassment.

"You're a beautiful woman. I like you and I want to keep on kissing you. I'm sorry if that makes your life more complicated, but I can't get all worked up about that. What I *do* care about is making you uneasy. I don't want to rush you or make you uncomfortable."

Her heart swelled until her chest ached. He liked her! He cared about her!

"I think you should kiss me now," she said.

"Bright girl," he murmured, right before his mouth claimed hers.

Billie wandered through an unfamiliar wing of the palace. It was her day off and while she'd planned on spending it in town, an unexpected rain storm had trapped her indoors.

It wasn't that she couldn't be out in the rain—although humidity did have a way of making her hair go flat—it was that the rain made her sad, which made her want to curl up and think, which under her current circumstances, was not a good thing. So she had decided to take Muffin for a long indoor walk through the wonders of the palace.

On the fourth floor, in the back, she found what

looked like an old schoolroom, complete with a few desks and a blackboard. Dozens and dozens of books filled several low bookcases. There were shelves with toys and plenty of windows to let in light.

While Muffin investigated corners, Billie walked into a large playroom. Several airplane models hung from the ceiling.

"Big mistake," she whispered as she touched the plastic prop on one. She had a good idea of who had painstakingly built them, and then hung them. Of course it was silly to spend time in the palace and expect to escape from thoughts of Jefri.

Still, she kept getting blindsided by thoughts and wishes and dreams. Funny how a whole month after that single night, she still remembered everything about their time together. She still missed him and was coming to grips with the concept that she might have made the mistake of falling in love with him.

If there were—

A soft sound caught her attention. Odd notes of music. She turned in the direction of the sound and walked down the corridor. The music got louder. She pushed open a door and found herself in an old-fashioned nursery. Emma, Reyhan's very pregnant wife, stood by a crib. She held a music box open on her hand.

"Hi," she said as Billie entered the room. "Exploring?"

"A little. It seemed that kind of day."

Emma glanced out the window. "Rain does that to me, too. Most people just want to curl up and read, but I get restless. Reyhan came in for some meetings and insisted I accompany him.''

Billie stared at the other woman's huge belly. ''When are you due?''

Emma grinned. ''In three weeks.''

''No doubt he's terrified you'll give birth while he's gone.''

''I promised I wouldn't, but did he listen?'' She closed the music box. ''Besides, I like it better at the desert palace. It's more like a house than this place.''

Billie laughed. ''You say that like it's a good thing.''

''Into the palace, huh?''

''Let's just say I love my bathroom more than I should.''

Emma nodded. ''It's very beautiful here. I'll admit that. I mean look at this nursery.''

Billie had to admit the room was amazing. There were mobiles and murals. A long changing table stood against one wall. The decors—blue and pale gray—screamed boy.

''So they really do hate women here,'' Billie said with a laugh.

''Nope. There's a fussy pink nursery next door. They certainly had the room to do both.''

''What are you having?'' Billie asked. ''Do you know?''

''I wanted to be surprised,'' Emma told her. ''Reyhan is convinced we're having a boy. Of course Sadik was sure of that as well, and Cleo had a girl.'' She touched her belly. "At this point I don't care if it's puppies, I just want it out."

Billie had never believed in biological clocks or pressure to start a family but at that second, she felt a distinct emptiness low in her belly.

Muffin scampered through the room, stopping long enough to sniff Emma's ankles before darting out the other door.

"She's doing well with all the cats," Emma said. "When I first heard you had a small dog, I'll admit I was worried."

"Me, too. But she gets along great with them. Sometimes she's gone for hours and I have no idea where she's been."

"Ah. A dog with a secret life. So you're enjoying your time here, too?"

Billie nodded. "Even without having a secret life. I love my work and the pilots in the air force are very talented."

"I've heard you regularly beat them. Is that true?"

"Oh, yeah. They love it."

Emma chuckled. "Why do I doubt that? How does Jefri take it?"

Billie tried not to react to his name. "With a lot of class. He was shocked at first, but he's gotten over it. Most guys simply can't handle it."

Emma looked at her. "Let me guess. Pilots are the only men you meet."

"Of course."

"It makes sense. If nothing else, life has a sense of

humor. So you're stuck with men who can't accept you're better than they are.''

"Much of the time.'' Although not with Jefri.

Don't think about that, she told herself. Don't think about him.

"What happens when you want to settle down?'' Emma asked.

"I don't know. For a while I thought I would have to give up my career and settle for something more traditional. But then I realized I can't stop being who I am simply to get married. I'll just have to keep looking until I find someone extraordinary enough to handle it.''

"He'll be lucky to have you.''

"Thanks.''

Emma opened her mouth, then closed it. "Okay, my thimble-sized bladder just started complaining. Excuse me while I waddle off in search of a bathroom. But before I go, Cleo and I are getting together for tea in a couple of hours. Please join us.''

"I'd like that.''

"Good. All right. This is me waddling.''

Emma waved as she walked out of the nursery. Billie moved in the other direction, toward the girl nursery. As promised, it was a paradise of pink and lace.

Billie closed her eyes and let the pain wash over her. If only…

If only Jefri had never spoken to his father. If only Tahira had never arrived. What would have happened? She would have fallen in love with him because that seemed to be her destiny. What about him?

She wanted to believe what she read in his eyes. She wanted to know that they could have been together, always. Happy, in love.

While she was living in her fantasy, she would imagine herself as pregnant as Emma, standing in this nursery, preparing it for her daughter. A daughter with her style and Jefri's eyes. She imagined him standing behind her, pulling her against him, whispering he loved her.

A single tear trickled down her cheek.

She called for her dog and when Muffin appeared, she picked her up and gathered her close.

''We have to go get pretty,'' she said. ''We're having tea with a couple of princesses.''

She brushed away the tear and vowed to stay strong. Wishing for the moon would only give her a cramp in her neck.

Chapter Fourteen

"You do not understand," Jefri said, both angry and frustrated with his brother.

Murat lounged on the sofa and sipped his scotch. "I understand perfectly. You're engaged to Tahira but are in love with Billie."

"Stating the problem again does not solve it."

"Agreed. You already know the solution. Dump Tahira."

"I cannot."

"I agree there will be some small scandal and she may be hurt, but if you love the other woman…"

Jefri glared at Murat. "Tahira would be ruined."

"She would recover."

"When did you get to be such a bastard about women?"

"I am not. I'm suggesting you be."

Jefri saw the amusement in his brother's eyes and wanted to throw his glass across the room. "You are not helping."

"I know, but in truth, you do not want help. You want a magical solution. There isn't one. You will have to choose. A moment of unkindness to Tahira or a lifetime of unhappiness with her. Although I have to admit, should you choose honor and duty, as you have been raised to, then you will turn your back on Billie. I, for one, would be most interested in helping her get over you."

Jefri didn't remember moving. One second he was pacing the length of his brother's luxurious suite, the next he had his brother by the shirtfront.

"She is mine," he growled.

Murat raised one eyebrow. "As bad as all that? Then I do not envy your choice."

Jefri released him and straightened. "I should not have done that."

"Probably not, but as I am not yet king, I won't have you beheaded. You might want to fix yourself another drink."

Jefri looked down at the glass he'd dropped on the carpet. "She makes me insane."

"Which one?"

"Both. I don't suppose…"

Murat smoothed the front of his shirt and shook his head. "Thank you, no. I have no interest in a child like Tahira. Although she seems nice enough, she is far too young and inexperienced."

"You would want a wife who was not a virgin?"

Murat frowned. "Of course not. I meant inexperienced in life. Tahira has much to learn and I am far too impatient to want to teach her."

Jefri picked up his glass and set it on the tray, then collected another and poured a second drink.

"Your time will come. Once I am engaged, Father will turn his sights to you."

"I suspect he already has," Murat said grimly.

"And after all this time, no one has caught your eye?"

His older brother grinned. "Many have caught my eye. None has held my attention."

"What of—"

Murat cut him off with a glare. "Do not say her name."

"It's been nearly ten years."

"I do not care if it has been twelve centuries. Her name is not to be spoken."

Jefri sipped his drink, but didn't speak. So even after all this time, his brother still did not want to hear Daphne's name. Interesting.

But his amusement faded as the ramifications of his brother's reaction sank in. Ten years after the fact Murat had not recovered from the woman who left him at the altar. Sadik and Reyhan loved their wives with a devotion that was almost embarrassing. Was it a family trait? Was he destined to love only one woman for the rest of his life? And if that was true, how could he survive while married to someone else?

* * *

Funny how destroying the Bahanian air force didn't make Billie feel any better. Still, it had been a good day. Jefri had held out nearly six minutes and his improved performance made her proud.

As she walked along the concrete bunker-style corridor on her way from the training center at the airport, she calculated how much longer was left on the training contract. While company personnel stayed to work the transition, Billie was assigned to flight training and that work would be finished in about three weeks. Nineteen days, to be exact. Not that she could decide if leaving would be a good thing or a bad thing.

On the plus side was the chance to reclaim her life. She could stop thinking about Jefri every waking moment and instead figure out what she wanted to do with herself. Was she happy? Were there other things she wanted to accomplish? Since that one fateful night, he had been her sole focus and she needed that to stop. The other plus would be an eventual decrease in pain. How nice not to have a constant ache in her chest. How nice to wake up looking forward to the day instead of dreading it.

On the negative side of things was the fact that once she left Bahania, she would never see Jefri again. At least not in person. No doubt she would see pictures in various magazines and maybe even on the news. Some cable channel would probably do a special on his wedding. Billie shook her head. She would not be watching that. Tahira was a sweet enough girl, but

Billie couldn't stand the thought of her married to Jefri.

At least Doyle was off her back. In the past few weeks he'd barely bugged her about her feelings for Jefri. In fact he'd been pretty great. Which made her wonder what was up.

"Doyle would say this was a situation he couldn't win," she said aloud, then grinned, when she realized he would be right. But as her brother, he didn't have to win.

Still smiling, she turned the corner and nearly stumbled when she saw the man walking toward her.

Even in the harsh fluorescent light, he looked gorgeous. Still dressed in his flight suit and boots, striding purposefully toward her, Prince Jefri of Bahania was the epitome of male grace and power.

She came to a stop in the center of the empty corridor. There was nothing to say to him, nothing that could be resolved, yet she couldn't seem to move. Her senses went on alert, her body trembled, her brain got fuzzy. All because he was near. If they'd been outdoors, she would have expected a couple of little birds to break into song.

He slowed as he approached, finally stopping in front of her. They stared at each other, gazes locked, bodies stiff. The air seemed to crackle with electricity. She tried to figure out something to say—something significant. In the end, she went for something easy.

"You did well today."

He nodded. "I have learned much from you."

"Now you'll be able to beat the bad guys at their own game."

"Should they attack the oil fields from the sky, we are prepared."

He looked gaunt, she thought. As if he hadn't been eating or sleeping. She could relate to both. Falling in love and then getting her heart broken was even better than getting the flu for losing a couple of pounds.

They were alone in the stone corridor. The tunnel-like space was so quiet, she would swear she could hear both their heartbeats.

"Are you—"

"I thought—"

They spoke at the same time. She ducked her head.

"You go," she said.

"No. You first. Please."

She looked at him, then wondered what she could possibly say. That she was sorry? She wasn't. Not for anything, except the obvious of his engagement. But even knowing what she knew now, she wouldn't *not* want to care. He'd touched her in a way that no man had, and that touching was about a lot more than just making love.

"I'm glad I met you," she whispered.

His expression tightened. "As am I. You are an extraordinary woman."

Neither of them stated the obvious. That if things had been different... But they weren't.

"Jefri, I—"

She couldn't say who moved first. Maybe she'd reached for him. Maybe he had taken a single step.

One second they were a good arm's length away from each other and the next they were in each other's arms, holding, pressing, kissing.

His mouth found hers, even as his arms wrapped around her body and drew her close. She went willingly, wishing she could climb inside and be a part of him forever. She wanted to feel his heat, his strength. She wanted to know all of him. Even as his mouth pressed against hers and she rediscovered the glory of kissing him, she was aware of his hard body, so different from her own.

Everything felt right, she thought as she tilted her head and parted her lips. He claimed her instantly, sweeping inside her mouth and touching her tongue with his.

He tasted as tempting as she remembered. They moved together in a dance designed to arouse and incite. She clutched his shoulders, hanging on to keep from falling. He pressed his fingers against her back, as if afraid she would bolt.

Had she been able to speak, she would have told him she never wanted to leave. That his arms would always be home. But to say the words meant breaking the kiss and that she couldn't do.

She wasn't sure how long they stood there, kissing, holding, wanting. Need built inside, but the sensation was bittersweet. Unfulfilled desire added a sharpness to her broken heart. She raised her hands to his head and tunneled her fingers through his hair.

And still they kissed—pressing, rubbing, wanting. He pulled back enough to nibble along her jaw. She sighed her pleasure as he kissed the sensitive skin on her neck. Their breathing increased until they were both nearly panting. Finally he drew back and cupped her face.

"Why do you leave me?" he asked, his voice thick with emotion.

She didn't ask how he knew she would go. She supposed there were those who would say, "Stay. See each other on the side. No one has to know." But that wasn't them.

"You have a life here and I belong somewhere else."

"The skies?" he asked.

"Pretty much."

He brushed his thumbs against her cheeks, wiping away tears she hadn't felt fall. Emotions filled his dark eyes.

"I love you, Billie," he said quietly. "With my heart and my soul. You have my heart in your possession. Treat it kindly."

She'd hoped he would admit he cared, but she'd never expected this. Tears flowed faster.

"I love you, too. More than anything." She sniffed, then stepped back and wiped her face. "This is so stupid."

"Our feelings?"

She laughed. "No. Me crying. For the first time in my life, a man is telling me he loves me and all I can do is cry."

"I am touched by your tears. You are not a woman who cries often."

That was true. "I try to save them for special occasions."

"Like this."

"I've never had an occasion like this."

She'd always thought that when she fell in love and that man loved her back, things would be happier than they were right now.

He moved close and kissed her.

"You are magic," he said. "I never expected to find someone like you. Not now."

Not while he was engaged.

His mouth twisted. He stepped back and clenched his hands into fists. "This is madness. I will go to her and tell her it is impossible. You are the one I want to be with. Not that child."

The words were exquisite torture, she thought, as the weight of the pain nearly drove her to her knees. That he would offer to do that for her.

She looked at him. More than offer, she thought. He meant it.

"You can't," she said, forcing herself to speak the truth while she still had the strength. "She loves you."

"She doesn't know what love is."

"Perhaps, but she cares as much as she can."

He dismissed her with a wave. Billie grabbed his arm.

"I've been spending time with her," she said. "You are all she speaks about. Every thought she has, everything she does is for you. She speaks about having your children, growing old with you. She talks about her duty to your country.'' She released him and ducked her head.

''I've tried to convince her otherwise,'' she admitted. ''Just little hints that she could have a different life if she wanted. A career. Freedom to travel. Meet other men.'' She squared her shoulders and forced herself to look at him. ''I'm not proud of that, but I did it.''

He pulled her close and kissed her. ''I'm sure you were kindness itself.''

''I was selfish. But the point is, Tahira was never interested. You're her world. You gave your word and we both have to respect that.''

''So the three of us are destined to unhappy lives?''

She didn't want to think of that. ''In time,'' she began.

He released her. ''In time what? I'll grow to love her? Knowing how I feel about you, do you believe I could love Tahira? Are there two women more different?''

''You have to try.''

''I see. And what about you? Will you go look for another man?''

Eventually, she thought. ''I'll have to. I want a husband and a family.''

Jefri turned away. She felt his pain because it was her own.

''I'm sorry,'' she whispered.

He shook his head. ''No. You are wise. I am the fool. I wish for what I cannot have and refuse to accept anything less.''

He turned back to her and reached into his pocket. "I have something for you. I have been carrying it around for a long time, not sure if I should give it to you. If you would accept."

He pulled out a wide, intricately carved gold bracelet. Different precious gems added to the pattern.

"They are very old and very rare. This one dates back to the early nine hundreds."

She took the stunning bracelet and turned it over in her hands. "There's no way to get it open."

He smiled. "That is part of the appeal. This is a version of a slave bracelet. The unlocking mechanism is hidden in the design. Some were made for the women in the harem. That way if they escaped, the bracelet marked them as a possession of the king. Others, like these, were made for the woman who possessed the king's heart. They offered protection, a free right of passage anywhere in the country. Those who aided her were rewarded."

He reached into his pocket again and held out a tiny key dangling from a delicate gold chain. "You see where the diamonds surround the sapphire?"

She found the spot on the bracelet and nodded.

"The key fits there. If you choose to wear the bracelet, know that you will always have a place to call home here. When you are ready, remove it."

She knew what he meant. When she loved another, she could take off the bracelet as a symbol of letting go.

Billie traced the wide gold band. The diamonds, sapphires and rubies glinted in the harsh lighting.

There was so much history in this single piece of jewelry. So much beauty.

"This should be on display in a museum," she said.

"I would prefer you to wear it."

She held out the band and he unlocked it. She slipped her wrist inside and snapped it closed. The cool metal fit perfectly.

Jefri slipped the chain over her head and she tucked the key under her blouse.

"Know you are protected," he said. "That if you become lost, all you have to do is ask and you will be directed to me. Whatever happens, wherever you go, there will always be a safe place for you here. When I am gone, my heirs will honor the promise of the bracelet until the day you draw your last."

He spoke the words as if they were a prayer…or a vow. They filled her heart with love and made her ache.

She took his hand in hers and leaned against him. "Maybe I'm not strong enough to do this. Maybe I want us to run away together and say the hell with the rest of the world."

He touched her lips with his fingertips. "You need only speak the words."

She glanced at the bracelet, then into his face. He meant it, she thought with amazement. If she asked him to go away with her, he would. He would turn his back on everything for her. The realization humbled her.

It was all there, she thought. Just out of reach. She

only had to grab for what she wanted and it would be
hers. But at what price? How many people would be
hurt or disappointed? Not just Tahira. What about
Jefri's family? How long would he be content to be
estranged from them? He was a prince and a sheik.
He could trace his lineage back over a thousand years.

"Speak the words," he repeated.

She drew in a breath for courage. "No."

Sadness darkened his eyes. "Are you sure?"

She wasn't, but she nodded because it was the right
thing to do.

"Please take me back to the palace," she whispered. "I'm going to need a long bath and a lot of
chocolate to get through the rest of the day."

He kissed her. "I will love you forever."

"I'll love you just as long."

They drove back to the palace in the back of a limo.
Billie snuggled close, resting her head on his shoulder.
She closed her eyes against the sights of the city she
had come to love, knowing that her days there were
dwindling. She could feel the weight of the bracelet
on her wrist and wondered how long it would be before she was willing to take it off.

She had a vision of herself as a very old lady, showing up at the palace and demanding refuge. Somehow
she knew that a handsome young prince would appear. He would speak gently, telling her of his father's
death and how Jefri had loved her to the end. Then
she would be taken to a pretty room where she would
live out her last.

It all sounded romantic, she thought. But in reality,

it sucked. Besides, she wanted to spend her last days surrounded by a large, loud family, not alone in a foreign country where no one knew her.

So in time, she would have to find the courage to put her love aside and go out and make a place for herself. There were good men out there. Men who could make her happy.

Or maybe she didn't need a man. Maybe she could start adopting kids and make a family that way. She had a lot to offer—a big heart and plenty of love. She could buy a house somewhere and settle down. As long as she was near an airport.

The limo slowed. She opened her eyes and saw they'd entered the palace grounds. Several guards approached the limo and motioned for the driver to stop. The rear door jerked open.

"Oh. Prince Jefri," the guard said. "My apologies. I'm under orders to search every vehicle."

Jefri stepped out. "What is going on?"

Billie followed him. There were dozens of guards everywhere. Up at the entrance to the palace, she saw the king talking with someone. It didn't look like a happy conversation.

"This can't be good," she said.

"I agree."

Jefri took her hand and led her toward his father. As they approached, the king dismissed the other man and turned to them.

"You are here at last," the old man said, looking both angry and worried.

"What has happened?" Jefri asked.

"Tahira is missing, and so is Doyle Van Horn."

Chapter Fifteen

Jefri followed his father into a private room off the entrance. It wasn't until he saw the king glance down that he realized he and Billie were still holding hands.

"When was Tahira last seen?" he asked, not concerned with what anyone might think, including the king.

Billie touched his arm. "I don't know what's going on here, but I know Doyle won't hurt her."

"Do not be concerned. I trust your brother as well." He turned his attention back to his father. "Are you sure they are together? Did they leave a note?"

"Tahira did." The king handed over a scrap of paper. "I cannot believe she has done this. Run away. Of all the ungrateful, disloyal actions…"

The king continued to rant, but Jefri ignored him. Instead he read the few lines Tahira had scrawled.

''I can't do this,'' she had written. ''Prince Jefri, I apologize for dishonoring you in this way, but I must escape. Please try not to hate me.''

Hate her? He shook his head. Hatred would require a depth of emotion he did not possess.

''She doesn't say anything about Doyle,'' Billie murmured. ''Maybe he's not with her.''

''They are together,'' the king said. ''She has shown a particular attachment to him. I did not mention anything because I thought it was a friendship, nothing more.'' He glowered. ''Young women cannot be trusted.''

Billie released Jefri's fingers and tucked her arm— the one with the bracelet—behind her.

''Are you saying they had a romance?'' Billie asked, sounding surprised.

''I am not sure how far things have gone. If he has defiled her...''

Billie paled. Jefri touched her arm.

''Nothing has happened yet.''

They watched as the king stalked to the other side of the room, picked up a phone and barked out orders for more guards to be sent into the city.

''He doesn't look happy,'' she whispered. ''I don't want to know the punishment for defiling a future princess.''

''The old laws have changed.''

''Great. But what if the new laws aren't any more forgiving?'' She stared at him. ''Are you angry?''

''That Tahira and Doyle may have run off together? No. I want her back and safe because she is my responsibility, but I have no emotional attachment past concern for her well-being.''

''If she and Doyle did, um, well, you know, what would happen?''

He understood the question. Would there still be an engagement?

''Let us first find out what has happened,'' he said, not wanting to wish for too much. If Tahira had fallen in love with Doyle, all of Jefri's problems were solved. But he had a feeling life wasn't going to be that simple.

He urged Billie to go up to her room and promised to notify her when he had word. Then he closed the door and faced his father.

''I am furious,'' the king said.

''Yes. You appear most upset. I am surprised.''

His father glared at him. ''Why? Tahira is like a daughter to me. To think she would be so disobedient injures me greatly. Plus there is the shame she visits on our family.''

''Yes. A wayward bride is fodder for the media.'' Jefri narrowed his gaze. ''You said you have seen them together?''

''What?'' His father paced to the window and stared out. ''A few times. In the garden. I thought nothing of it.''

Jefri found that difficult to believe. ''Tahira might be eighteen chronologically, but in experience, she is still very much a child. Did you not consider that Doyle Van Horn could easily seduce her?''

"I trusted him! I allowed him to live in my palace and in return I expected him to respect his place."

"But to put temptation in his path like that."

His father turned on him. "What are you saying?"

"That you could have stopped this some time ago, and yet did not. I wonder why."

The king turned back to the window without speaking. An idea formed in Jefri's mind and he could not seem to shake it.

Was this all part of a plan on his father's part? Not Tahira's arrival—Jefri himself had set that disaster in motion—but the rest of it? Under normal circumstances the king would never allow a future bride to one of his sons to spend afternoons alone with another man, let alone enough time for them to plan an escape. Then there was his father's insistence that Jefri marry Tahira. That she would be destroyed if he broke off the engagement. Had that been a ploy to make him realize the depth of his feelings about Billie?

"You are a wily old man," Jefri said with a shake of his head.

His father stared at him. "What are you talking about?"

"You have too much time on your hands. First you played Reyhan with Emma, insisting they spend time with each other before you would grant them their divorce. You suspected they were still in love and forced them into each other's company until they could not deny what they felt."

His father smiled. "What makes you think Reyhan

was the first?'' he asked before walking out of the room.

Jefri stared after him. Had his father played a hand in Sadik's marriage to Cleo? Had he been toying with Jefri as well?

He was torn between fury at the old man's meddling and pity for Murat—the last single brother.

Two hours later a shamefaced Tahira and a pale but defiant Doyle were returned to the palace. The king chose to meet them in the royal chamber where the large throne and formally dressed guards were designed to shake the confidence of the strongest of men.

Jefri stood at his father's right hand and glared down at Doyle. Whether or not Jefri wanted to marry Tahira, she was his responsibility and he did not take the situation lightly.

''You were a guest in this house,'' Jefri told Doyle. ''You were treated with honor and expected to act in kind. Instead you have taken one of our greatest treasures for your own personal pleasures.''

Doyle frowned. ''She's not a vase or a picture. She's a woman.''

''Exactly. A special young woman with great potential. She is not yours, Doyle Van Horn. You had no right.''

Tahira choked on a breath and threw herself in front of Doyle.

''Don't hurt him. Please, Prince Jefri. I know what

I did was wrong and unforgivable, but don't hurt him.''

Doyle put his arm around her. ''Don't apologize. You did nothing wrong.''

''In that you are correct,'' Jefri said. ''You are the one charged here.''

Tahira blanched. ''No! You can't. Please. I beg you.''

Doyle stood straight and strong. ''I'm not afraid of you.''

''You should be,'' the king said sternly. ''We have kept the peace here for over a thousand years and we have done that through the use of fair laws that apply to all. No one has the right to kidnap an innocent young woman for his own debased pleasures.''

''I didn't kidnap her,'' Doyle ground out through clenched teeth. ''I was trying to help her escape.'' He looked at Jefri. ''You don't want her. You can barely stand her and you'll never love her. So why the hell are you insisting on marrying her?''

He turned to Tahira. ''You're just as bad. Tell him the truth.''

She ducked her head. ''I am here to do Prince Jefri's bidding.''

Doyle swore. ''Tahira, for once would you just say what you want? Nothing horrible will happen. I promise.''

Tears filled her eyes. ''They're going to kill you.''

''We're not that savage,'' the king said. ''But there must be a reckoning.''

Jefri had heard enough. He stepped down and took

Tahira's hand. "Come, child," he said kindly. "We will speak in private."

As he led her out of the room, he glanced back at the guards. "Hold him until I return."

He showed Tahira to a small antechamber behind the throne. There he settled her on a chair and got her a glass of water. When she had the tears under control, he pulled up a chair next to her and sat down.

"Are you all right?" he asked, careful to keep his voice calm and gentle.

She nodded, clutching the glass in both hands. "Doyle didn't hurt me. You have to believe me."

"I do. I know he didn't carry you off against your will. You wanted to go with him, didn't you?"

Her eyes widened as she nodded.

"Over the past few weeks, you have become friends."

"Yes."

Good. His father had been telling the truth about that. Now to get the rest of the information.

"Do you love him?"

She shrank back in her seat. "No, Prince Jefri. No. I would never... We haven't..."

"I believe you, but you do care for him?"

She blushed and stared at the glass. "Doyle is very kind to me. When we talk, he makes me laugh. We talk about different things. The world. There is so much I haven't seen."

"And you want to see it?"

She nodded.

"Without me?"

Her breath caught and she raised her face. "You are so wonderful. You have honored me in so many ways and I am grateful."

"Tahira, I am not interested in your gratitude. I want your happiness. I was led to believe that you desired this marriage above all things, yet I now think that is not true. Would it not be better to simply tell me what is in your heart rather than risk a life of unhappiness because you are momentarily afraid?"

"You sound like Doyle."

"Apparently he has occasions of true wisdom."

That made her smile. She sucked in a deep breath. "I do not want to be married," she said, speaking quickly as she tightened her grip on the glass.

He took it from her before she snapped it and cut herself. Relief swept through him. He thought he might drown in the sensation. His future suddenly lay before him, a bright road of promise. But he had to be sure.

"What do you want?" he asked.

"I would like to study fashion design. In Paris. That's where Doyle and I were going. We weren't running away to be together." She blushed again. "Not exactly. He was going to help me find a place to stay and look into school."

"You speak French?" he asked.

"Yes. And Italian. They make lovely shoes there."

He smiled. "So I have heard." He took her hand in his. "Tahira, you have honored me with your loyalty. I am sorry you felt you had to sneak away to achieve your heart's desire. That was never my intent.

I would very much like to help you get settled and find a school.''

He would take care of her financially, as well, but there was no need to discuss that now.

''You're not angry?'' she asked, sounding stunned.

''No. I am delighted.'' More than that, but again not a conversation they needed to have.

She flung herself at him. ''Thank you, Prince Jefri. Thank you a thousand times.''

''I appreciate your enthusiasm at not becoming my wife.''

She giggled. ''You know I don't mean it that way.''

''I do.''

She straightened and stared at him. ''About Doyle. Please don't hurt him. He didn't do anything wrong.''

''So you keep saying.'' He pretended to consider the matter. ''I suppose you want to keep seeing him.''

Tahira nodded eagerly.

''He is several years older than you,'' Jefri reminded her. ''That could present some problems.''

''I can handle them.''

Her confidence made him smile. ''As you wish. But your visits with Doyle will be chaperoned for the time being. Until you find your place in the world.''

Tahira hugged him again. He held her briefly, knowing there was somewhere else he would rather be.

Billie paced the length of her suite, pausing every few minutes to listen for footsteps. When she finally heard them she raced to the door and jerked it open.

''What happened?'' she demanded as Jefri entered the room and pulled her into his arms.

''I love you,'' he said as he kicked the door closed and pressed his mouth to hers.

Billie surrendered to his embrace, to the feel of his body pressing against hers.

''I love you, too,'' she murmured, barely able to speak as she clung to him.

He bent low and swept her up in his arms. Muffin looked up from a cushion on the sofa, yawned and went back to sleep. He laughed.

''Good. Because you are not invited.'' Then he walked into the bedroom and closed the door there.

''What happened?'' Billie asked again as he set her on her feet and reached for the buttons on her blouse.

''Tahira wishes to study fashion design in Paris. She has no interest in marrying me and seems to have some fondness for Doyle.''

He pulled the blouse open and gazed at her breasts. ''You are so beautiful.''

Warmth flooded her. She tugged his shirt free of his trousers. ''You're not half-bad yourself. So there's no engagement?''

''Not anymore. I suspect my father knew what was going on the whole time and that he played me to get me to see how much you mattered.''

''You're kidding.''

''No.''

He bent down and claimed her with a kiss that left her weak with longing. He stroked her body, removing clothing as he went. She did her best to help take off his, but she was continually distracted by things like his mouth on her breasts or his fingers between her legs.

He touched her and loved her until she couldn't think, couldn't breathe, couldn't do anything but feel.

Poised between her thighs, he stared into her eyes.

"Stay," he breathed. "Stay with me."

She lost herself in his dark eyes. "Of course I'll stay."

"I want you to marry me. Have my children. Be a part of me, a part of my country. I cannot survive without you."

Tears burned in her eyes. She blinked them away. "I love you, Jefri. I can't imagine being anywhere else."

"Then you'll say yes?"

"Yes. For always."

He plunged into her, claiming her with an intimate pleasure that swept her into another dimension.

Later, when they could both breathe easily, she snuggled close.

"I guess I never have to take this off now," she said, holding up her wrist and admiring the bracelet.

"You will never have to worry," he told her. "My people will love you as I do. This will be your home. The palace and the skies."

She rested her chin on his chest and looked at him. "So you're not going to get all weird and tell me I have to give up flying?"

"Of course not. You belong with the clouds. The difference is now I will join you there."

"I'll still beat you in a dogfight. Don't think marrying me is going to change that."

He laughed. "I now have a lifetime to practice. Eventually I will win."

"In your dreams."

His smile faded. "You are my dream. My fantasy. For always."

She sighed. "You're really good at this."

"I am very much in love."

"Me, too. In fact—"

A faint scratching caught her attention. "Oh, give me a sec. Muffin needs to go out. I just have to open the suite door."

Billie stood, slipped on Jefri's shirt then walked out to the living room where she let out her dog. Then she hurried back to the bedroom.

"Where were we?" she asked as she slipped back under the covers.

Jefri reached for her. "I believe we were here."

Muffin trotted down the long corridors of the palace, ignoring all the cats she passed. At the large, carved doors she waited while the guard let her in, then she hurried over to the big sofa opposite the window.

"There you are," the king said as he patted the cushion next to his. "Did you not see? I told you things would work out."

Muffin jumped up next to the king. The white cat there shifted to make room, then began to groom Muffin's face. The small dog sighed with pleasure.

"Only Murat is left," the king said. "But not to worry. I have given the situation much thought and I have come up with an excellent plan. Would you like to hear it?"

* * * * *

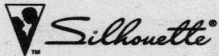

Coming December 2004 from

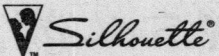
Silhouette®

SPECIAL EDITION™

and reader favorite

Sharon De Vita

RIGHTFULLY HIS

SE#1656

Max McCallister had given Sophie the greatest gift—
the children her husband, his brother, hadn't been able
to give her. But not long after Max became sperm donor
and Sophie gave birth, his brother died. After years of
hiding his feelings for the woman he'd always secretly
loved, had the time finally come for Max to claim
what was rightfully his—Sophie and
his twin daughters?

Available at your favorite retail outlet.

If you enjoyed what you just read,
then we've got an offer you can't resist!

Take 2 bestselling love stories FREE!
Plus get a FREE surprise gift!

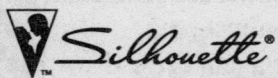

COMING NEXT MONTH